DEEP DESIRES

CHARLOTTE STEIN

Mischief
An imprint of HarperCollins*Publishers*
77–85 Fulham Palace Road,
Hammersmith, London W6 8JB

www.mischiefbooks.com

A Paperback Original 2013

First published in Great Britain in ebook format by
HarperCollins*Publishers* 2012

Copyright © Charlotte Stein 2012

Charlotte Stein asserts the moral right to
be identified as the author of this work

A catalogue record for this book is
available from the British Library

ISBN-13: 9780007534906

Set in Sabon by FMG using Atomic ePublisher from Easypress

Find out more about HarperCollins and the environment at
www.harpercollins.co.uk/green

CONTENTS

Chapter One

I don't mean to keep spying on him, as he strips out of his clothes. But the thing is, I just don't expect it. No one could expect it. I've seen him in hallways and around The Courtyard looking so strange and still and boxed in, in his always buttoned overcoats and his too thick glasses and that face of his, as expressionless as a glacier.

He just doesn't look the type to have the body he does. He looks like the type to be doughy underneath, as flaccid and pale as undercooked fish, but once he's gotten down to his queerly exciting underwear – long in the leg and somehow skintight – I'm transfixed.

I actually stop pretending I'm drawing the curtains and let myself linger on the taut planes of his body, so perfectly visible beneath that clingy material. And those thighs, God, those thighs. Where did he get those thighs from? And how do they look so good and thick and solid beneath what is, essentially, a pair of longjohns?

He should look ridiculous. He *is* ridiculous. Mrs Hoffman from 3F calls him the Serial Killer, because no one knows where he works or what he does, and Kayla from 4D swears blind she saw him opening and shutting his door three times, like something she saw once on *CSI*.

But I don't know. I don't know about him, and I want to know even less about their furtive gossip sessions around the pool that sits in the middle of our courtyard.

It's sitting there right now, giving a dull blue glow to this thing I'm definitely not doing. Like a neon lamp flashing stop stop stop, before it gets as far as, say, him taking off that long-sleeved woollen top.

Which he does, while I clutch the curtain into one sweaty fist and pretend this isn't affecting me at all. Because it definitely isn't. It's having no more effect on me than seeing him peel an orange did the other day.

I just looked out of my window, down onto his window across the courtyard, and there he was. Sat at a table, eating a piece of fruit. No big deal.

Only it is a big deal, because now he's peeling something else altogether. He's peeling himself, and after a moment I can see the solid mass of his pectoral muscles.

I can see the nearly honeyed hue of his skin, pale from the pathetic weather up here in Darkly Falls, but buttery because of something uniquely *him*.

Though his skin tone isn't the thing that draws my eye. It isn't even the sight of the rough scratch of hair all over his chest and belly, or the thought of how many crunches he had to do before his abs hardened into that exact shape.

It's the way he puts his thumb and forefinger to his lips, licks, and then slicks that wetness over one tight nipple.

Lord, I don't even know what to say about that. The urge to slam the curtain shut wells up in me, bright and strong, but the questions filling my head win out. Questions like:

Do men actually do things like that?

I can't quite believe that they do, given the information I've previously been given by Sid, my last unfortunate foray into relationships – *I got no feeling there, just suck my fucking cock,* etc. – and yet there it is, right in front of me. A man, rubbing and pinching and playing with one of his own nipples. And then even more incriminating, his mouth opens slightly – as though touching himself that way feels like the best thing in the world.

I can almost *hear* him moaning, through the glass. Though, of course, that's what makes me realise what he's going to do.

I realise it before I let my gaze travel downwards, to the thick, heavy bulge between his legs. I realise it before he tugs at the waistband of those ridiculous longjohns, and everything in me screams, look away, look away *now*.

I think I even go as far as to take a step backwards, but it's far too little and far too late. Besides, if I move too much he'll undoubtedly see me, even with my apartment all dark like this and his all light. He'll make out my silhouette, or the slide of the curtains, and then I'll always be the woman across the courtyard who watched him ease his underwear down over his heavy-boned hips, to reveal his glorious cock.

Because, by God, it *is* glorious. I've seen enough terrible porn while huddled beneath the safety of my sheets to know what a glorious one should look like, even if I've never viewed one in reality. In reality, I've seen short stunted ones and big hairy ones and ones that look as though they belong on someone as muted and strange as he is. But I've never seen a cock like the one he actually has.

He isn't cut for a start. A man as tidy seeming as him should be cut, but apparently his sexual self doesn't give a shit about things like that. His sexual self is as generous as he seems mean, as lush as he is contained.

It's quite a revelation. But not as much of a revelation as the *size* of him. I want to glance at my wrist just to make a comparison, even though that's ridiculous. No one has a cock as thick as a wrist, and even if they did they wouldn't be living in some godforsaken apartment block called The Courtyard, waiting for neighbours to spy on them.

He should be out there fucking someone, I think. Fucking some tight-bodied, thin-lipped girl with his thick, deliciously curved cock.

Is it such a crime that I'm picturing it right now? The girl with her legs spread wide, that big, solid thing easing in and out of her wet, willing hole. Him losing some of that strange, serial-killer control until he makes that noise for her – the one I can't quite hear.

Lord. Why am I like this?

I don't even know what *this* is, to be honest. I only know that my nipples have stiffened beneath the stupid Mickey Mouse printed material of my pyjama top, and, when I move even the tiniest fraction, I can feel how wet I suddenly am – wetter than I've been in a long, long time. Wetter than I ever was for Sid, and his constant gruelling demands that I just enjoy it, that I'd better fucking enjoy it, that if I don't enjoy it he's going to make me with his fists.

And it's for *him*. The Serial Killer. The guy with the eyes that always seem as though they're covered in gauze. The one I'm urging to masturbate with my mind, even as my sanity begs him not to. *Don't*, I think, at no one in particular.

But then he strokes one hand over himself, long and slow, and I forget I've ever had any thoughts about anything at all, ever.

It just looks so *good*. The way he does it, all nice and easy as though he's got all the time in the world and he's absolutely not stood in front of his own window right now. In fact, I think he's kind of *leaning* against his window, which seems even ruder somehow. He's pushing into the glass, one hand stroking and stroking over his cock, until the flesh there is as slick as I feel.

I don't mind admitting that the sight excites me. It makes me think of dirty things, like maybe he got some lube before he started, and is now spreading it all over himself. Or possibly he licked his palm when I wasn't looking, and all that slipperiness is his spit, getting worked and worked into his stiff cock.

Though neither of these ideas is as hot as the one that occurs a moment later: that maybe it's his own lubrication. He's so turned on that he's leaking thin streamers of pre-come, and, if I was just a little closer, I'd be able to see it clearly.

I want to be closer. I want to take that cock in my mouth, and suck until he's even slicker. I want him to moan for me the way I know he's moaning now – head back, mouth open, body vibrating with the kind of pleasure I've never experienced.

His hand tightens on his cock to the point where I'm

sure it should hurt, but the roll of his hips says otherwise. He's practically fucking his fist now, lips moving around words I long to hear. Are they dirty, those words? Is he saying a stream of hot things to himself, to urge his orgasm on?

I like to think so, but it's hard to tell, when it's someone like him. I can't imagine him saying stuff like *yeah, suck me off, baby*, but then again I could never have imagined him doing what he's doing.

Fucking himself, where anyone could see. I mean, it's three o'clock in the morning, but that doesn't mean anything. The drunk girl from 9G often stumbles home around this time, and I bet she'd have to walk right past his window to get to the entrance. Even if she'd have to stand on tiptoe to see in, it's still too exposed.

Unless maybe he *wants* to be exposed, to her. Maybe she stumbles through the courtyard and then right into his apartment, to do all the things I'd never dare to: suck him and fuck him and let him come all over her, God, I want him to come all over her.

He's going to do it now, I can tell. His hips are jerking and he's biting his lip and the head of his cock looks so red and swollen, as though he's just about to burst. Go on, I think, go on, as he rubs himself faster and faster, thumb sliding over the slick tip on every upstroke, body shuddering and shuddering.

I can almost *taste* his climax, can almost see it arcing

from the head of his swollen cock, but it seems as though it's never going to come. He can't get at it, in a way that makes me just ache for him. My entire body feels strung taut and raw, but it gives this one extra pulse for him. This little shiver of something that gets me closer to the glass, that makes me dare to drop my bunched hand one inch closer to my breast.

It must be as bad for him as it is for me. My nipples just feel so stiff, so tense with pleasure that I'm not willing to spill, and between my legs there's that same sensation magnified a thousand times.

Liquid is soaking into my little sleep shorts. My sex swells against the material, tight and aching for release, but I can't, I can't. I'm in darkness, but I still can't.

It's too much. I have to be satisfied with watching and imagining a million dirty things – like him finally spurting all over my spread cunt – and even those are too much. They make me a pervert, a person who could rightly be called a voyeur, though I confess I didn't really know what being a voyeur meant, until now.

It's like I'm inside his skin, as his cock leaps and his entire body ripples, that firm hand of his slowing a little on his cock as the first thick pulse of come eases out over his fist.

The second is stronger and he seems to go rigid when it hits – as though the pleasure's too much. And then the third spasm hits and it *is* too much, it's definitely too much, because he puts his free hand to his mouth and bites down so hard I feel an answering pang of pleasure go through me.

It's so intense that for a moment I'm sure I've climaxed too. I'm absolutely drenched down there, and all of these little aftershocks are jolting through me – though, when he finally moves away from the window, I know I haven't gone over.

I know because this great aching void opens up in me, unresolved, unsatisfied, untouched. And though I try to step back and think of other things – the shift at the grocery store I've got tomorrow, the one dirty tape I possess that I could masturbate to now, if I so chose – I can't.

It's too late. He has me now.

Chapter Two

I see him in the hallway getting his mail, but shamefully pretend I don't. I go as far as to pretend we're actually strangers, and have never so much as exchanged a nod of the head. Instead of the truth, which is still utmost in my mind:

I watched you masturbate last night.

I think the words at his back, as he turns and begins to sift through whatever letters he's received. Probably bills, I'm sure. Maybe a leaflet from a charity he donates to. Possibly a subscription to a really innocent and normal magazine.

Like *Horny Voyeurs Monthly*.

Because that's what I am, isn't it? I stepped out of my life of supermarket working and TV watching and dying a little inside every day, and I watched with bated breath as a man did something sexual to himself, in the ostensible privacy of his home.

Even though it's not really privacy at all now. I mean, he had to know that wasn't private. He must have understood that I could see him, that anyone could have seen him, even though I rarely see an open curtain in this place.

But when I push those words into his back and he doesn't even turn, I start to think otherwise. He didn't secretly want someone to see him. And whatever connection I'm imagining between us is just that: imaginary. None of this is actually real. I'm just a loser who spied on someone, and he's actually a really cool guy who has an amazing job, like software developer.

Those glasses he wears? They're not dorky. They're ... they're *hipster*.

And that's what I'm thinking when he closes the metal door of his little post box – not three times, like Kayla claimed – and starts in my direction. Hipster, I think, cool and unattainable and awesome, as he strides towards me in slow motion. Those eyes, like something blurred beneath a mist-covered pane of glass. Those cheekbones – God, did he have cheekbones like that before? I could reach out and cut my finger on them, if I ever dared to do anything like touch him.

Which, of course, I won't. I can't even bring myself to

meet his gaze when it flicks to me for just the barest second – like maybe he can't help himself. He wants to be aloof, I think. He needs to pretend that all of this is just something I dreamed up, one night when I couldn't sleep.

Only that one darting look says otherwise. It flashes out of him, as bright and sharp as he is dark and blunted. And once he's made it all the way to the end of this stifling green hallway – like a tunnel in a funhouse that doesn't exist – I take that one surreptitious glance and bury it down deep inside me.

I keep it close, for all the times I've wanted something like that and been denied.

He saw me.

And I know beyond a shadow of a doubt that I have seen him.

* * *

The next time I dare to look, I'm disappointed. Of course I am. He's closed his curtains, like a sign: I know what you did. And I don't *like* it.

Even though I know that's completely irrational. If I accept that he knows what I did, I have to also accept that he did it on purpose. He could have stopped once he realised I was watching – and yet here we are. Trapped in our places. Him with his curtains drawn, me wishing they weren't.

Though I understand it's not just because of the dirty things now. It's not just because of his gorgeous body and his filthy actions, I swear it's not. It's those eyes, burning out at me. It's that look that lingered long after the event, so furtive and ... and complicit, somehow. I lie in bed thinking of the weight of that gaze, and when I actually entertain the idea of putting my hand between my legs it's with his face in mind.

Would he stare at me like that as he fucked me? With that kind of intensity? I don't know and obviously will never be privy to it, but that's beside the point, isn't it? I can fantasise. For the first time in my life, I can actually fantasise about a real, living, breathing person and not panic.

I'm safe, behind the glass. I can lie on my stomach and press a pillow between my thighs, then imagine him taking me like that, haunches up like an animal. With Sid, it was never like that. It was always face to face so that he could slap me as we did it, but I'm not sure my blue-eyed Serial Killer would be that way.

He'd probably just chop up my body and put it in the freezer.

Or maybe he'll simply leave his curtains open, when I least expect it.

It's the seventh day since it happened, and I've almost started thinking it was a dream. And then I wake up twisted on my side, foggy with images I don't want to

Charlotte Stein

have in my head, and there's a glow seeping into my apartment. I can see it just edging its fingers across the carpet, like the light of a convenience store after you've just trekked ten miles through a barren desert.

I think of the *Rocky Horror Picture Show* – that song they sing when they see the castle and think everything's going to be OK – and then I heave myself out of bed like a zombie and stumble across to that light.

It can't be helped. I'm dying of thirst. I'm drowning in desperation. I have to hang on to my own curtains just to keep myself standing, and then I see him. He's in the window, just like before. On the same day, too, I realise, which practically makes this some sort of ritual. I was silly to doubt him, or imagine he thought badly of me.

He just likes to do it on the same day every week, the way he likes to do everything. The orange, I remember, always gets peeled at the same time. And he picks his mail up at certain intervals – maybe when it's safe to come out of his lair.

And so it follows that he stands in front of his window half-naked, at the previously allotted time. He's even wearing the same garb he did before – those queer long-johns, so tight over his every bulge and curve.

Though there's a subtle difference.

He's not stood up. He's sat at that little table in front of his window, and he isn't staring straight forward, like an automaton playing out a role.

He's staring up at my window. I know he is. I know he is even though I kind of lean forwards and look up, expecting to somehow see a prettier woman in the apartment above ... Or maybe she's below me? Yeah, maybe she's doing an exotic dance for him in the apartment below me, and, once she's done, *that's* when he masturbates.

For her. Not for me.

And the message he's scrawled on his window in lipstick?

That's for her, too.

Your turn now, it says, and I can't help admiring his gall. I admire his lettering, too – as neat as he seems, as ordered, in spite of the ink he's used. I'm fairly certain it's lipstick – so red and garish, glaring in the backwash of that strange light from his apartment – but of course I can't fathom why.

He seems more the sort to have made a neatly printed sign in Microsoft Word, with an elegant and stark border and a font that can be registered clearly. *It's your turn now*, it would say, but maybe with a *sincerely, The Serial Killer* after it, instead of what I get.

Which is nothing.

I'm allowed that much – no names, no promises, no pleases or thank yous – and even that much seems like a stretch. I didn't realise he knew how to talk. That wasn't a part of the programme when he first introduced me to it.

I'm just supposed to watch, I think. That's my role: to watch him peel out of his clothes and abuse himself. He has to know that I can't do the same for him in return, no matter how tightly he folds those massive arms or how closely he watches me be this shadow in the window.

Because that's what I'll look like, isn't it? My light isn't on. He can maybe make out the wispy white corner of my nightgown, and possibly the edge of one of my arms. I'm a ghost made up of higgledy-piggledy random parts, which he's probably pieced together in completely the wrong order.

In his head, he's given me a slimmer build, smaller breasts, daintier feet and hands. That glimpse he caught of me in the hall ... it hasn't helped him. He probably just saw my eyes, black as night and twice as lovely as the rest of me, and made his suppositions from there.

Now I'm some exotic gypsy, ready to play for him. I'm not a girl who let some man degrade her for a year, before breaking free into absolute nothingness. Into this place, chill as an arctic night. Into this life, monotonous and samey but ultimately safe.

I don't have to worry in this life.

Or, at least, I *didn't* have to worry. Until now.

Which is probably why I slowly draw my curtain back across the window, and return to my bed. And then, once I'm there, I sleep the numbing sleep of the dead.

Deep Desires

* * *

The words are gone by the next night, and I know what that means all too well. I missed my chance. I didn't do what I was told, so now I have to pay. Of course, the price in this situation is far less than the ones I've paid in the past. It's just a withdrawal of a promise, an erasure of possible delights and pleasures that I'm sure I didn't want anyway.

Yet it stings all the same. I'm back to being just a checkout girl, who doesn't dance with a Serial Killer in the pale moonlight. I'm nothing, I think, as I stare down at his sullenly dark window.

And then the light in his apartment abruptly goes on, and suddenly my heart is beating like a trapped bird in my chest. There doesn't even seem to be any build up to it, either. One second I'm silent and still inside, the next second my pulse is trying to leap out of my body. I can lie and lie and lie to myself, it seems, and pretend that I don't care whether I'm nothing or not, but my body tells the truth.

It means something to me that he comes to the window half-dressed, sweatpants slung so low on his hips a breath could knock them down. It means that he didn't care whether I did anything for him or not.

He's still going to do anything for me.

And he does. *Anything*, I mean. I'm not sure I've ever

17

seen a guy do the things he offers me, right there in his window where anyone could see. In all honesty, I've never even seen a guy masturbate, or be vulnerable, or give a single thing without taking. So this ... this is right out.

He puts his fingers in his mouth, slow, slow. Like he's putting on a show for me, and knows it. He even knows the things I want to see – like the glimpse of his tongue I get between those two filthy fingers. It's a promise, I think, some sort of seductive version of a guy suggesting a very specific sex act, but different to that, too.

I don't think of guys in bars, waggling their tongues. I think of that slippery thing just easing over my swollen clit, and then suddenly my hand is on the window, holding me up. The glass is ice cold beneath my palm and barely any comfort at all, but that's OK. I don't need comfort here.

I need him to keep doing whatever he's going to do.

Though of course it isn't what I expect. At first it goes that way. He slides that hand down under the waistband of his sweatpants, and I can see him stroking over the thick shape beneath the material. I can even recall exactly what that heavy thing looked like, all slippery at the tip and swollen, most of it the same honey colour as his gorgeous body.

But he only lingers there a little while. He strokes once, maybe twice, enough to get his eyes to stutter closed. I see that lewd little tongue come out to wet his lips – those lips like a bow, notching an arrow straight at my heart – and then his hand slides around inside that secretive material. I mean, you can just about see what he's doing. The cloth is thin enough to make out his knuckles, shifting like a formless face beneath a veil.

But it's all just hidden enough that you can imagine you're seeing things. It's a magic trick, an illusion, and I'm holding my breath for some kind of big reveal. I've clenched my fist into the centre of my chest again, as that hand makes its way around his body and oh God, oh God.

He's not going to do *that*, is he? Does he know I'm not even sure what *that* is? I've heard whispers. I've seen movies. I know that people don't just put peg A into slot B. Yet even so I'm trembling and mesmerised, watching him touch himself in this unbearably intimate way.

It's worse than if he were naked. I have to imagine it all instead – though all my imagination can come up with is him stroking slow and wet between the cheeks of his arse, teasing himself the way that I sometimes tease myself. I don't go in, you know. I don't do that. I just rub over that tightly clenched hole while I play with my clit, and usually when I do my mind goes elsewhere.

But he keeps my mind right here.

His mouth is open now, and his eyes are closed. I can still tell what expression he's wearing behind them, however. I'd know mindless pleasure anywhere, having seen it faked a million times – which makes me think this is just a show, for a little while. He's squirming around in a way men never do, and I can almost hear his moans as he pretends to work a finger into his tight little asshole ... but none of it's actually real.

Until he jerks and sinks his teeth into his lower lip, and I see the spreading darkness on the front of his sweatpants.

I may be dumb and mute and foolish, but I know what that means. He's just worked himself to a shuddering climax on those probing, searching fingers, and I missed half of it, imagining it was all a masquerade. I missed the strangest, most exciting event of my life, because I couldn't believe it was real.

It's not a surprise.

* * *

I've always thought the fluorescent lights in the store where I work were very bright. Unbearably bright. I go home still squinting from their glare, and remain so even in the closed-off darkness of The Courtyard.

And yet somehow they seem dimmer today than they did before. They've lost power in the time between me looking into the Serial Killer's eyes and right now. They've turned to a low and crackling blue, somewhere in the distance of my life.

Though it isn't just them. The candy-bright wrappers that line the shelves seem to have faded; my apron is more worn and withered than it once was. I take the thing off the moment I get home, and marvel at the thinness of the material, the patheticness of the pattern. Is this what I've been wearing all this time? This chequered thing, as limp and lifeless as a body found floating in the pool?

I don't know, but it feels good to get the apron off. And it feels even better to stand beneath the groaning pipes of my crookedly tiled shower and wash all of that away. When I'm done, I put on the long nightgown – the one I cleaned and dried this morning, in the rumbling machines that shudder around the washroom – and go to the window.

By the time I do, my heart is already hammering in my chest. These little meetings – they could still be a dream of some sort. Maybe I think I'm awake when I'm asleep, and asleep when I'm awake. Maybe he's changed his mind, and finds me a dull sort of creature, now.

It's not as though he's wrong after all. I'm so dull I'm almost crying, torn with tension over something as simple as opening the curtain. What if he's there, oh God, what if he's there? And even worse: what if he's not? I don't think I could take it if he wasn't, though, when I wrench the curtain back and his window is dark and silent, I'm surprisingly calm.

This is how things are supposed to be, I think. I can't be disappointed about something that shouldn't really happen to me. It's not even all that big a deal, really – just a little game played through two windows in the middle of the night. No one would ascribe it some profound meaning, or pin so many of their hopes on it continuing.

Yet my heart still jerks in my chest when I catch a glimpse of something stirring through the darkness. A flash of white, I think it is – the way my nightgown probably looks – and then I see the now familiar shape of him more clearly.

He's sat in a chair in front of the table that sits below his window. And everyone now and then he'll reach forward for a glass he's placed on the wood, in this deliberate sort of way – like a rich man in a velvet club, waiting for the girl to come out.

I'm the girl, I think. He's waiting and watching for me, even though I can't see his eyes to confirm. There's a black band of darkness over them like a blindfold made of nothing, and, I have to say, it makes me feel easier about turning on the light. His eyes are as sightless as the dozens of curtain-covered windows that stare down at me, so what does it matter if I just do this thing?

I barely feel exposed at all once I have. I'm electric instead, trembling with a kind of excitement I've never felt before. Different points of my body call to me, call to me, like a siren song. And I go to them. I do.

I stroke my breasts through material that had seemed thick before but now feels gossamer light. In fact, it's so light I can make out the exact shape of my stiff nipples beneath, so taut and spiky I can hardly bear to touch them. And the response I get when I do ... oh God. The sensation that radiates outwards as I circle first one, then the other ...

It's enough to make me gasp without thinking, and then of course my face heats directly afterwards. Of course it does – I'm not supposed to make a sound. I'm not supposed to be noisy and uncouth, and I think of that restriction all the way up until the moment of realisation:

It doesn't actually matter if I am.

After all, I'm alone right now. There's no one else in here with me. I could scream and no one would hear me, though I'm nowhere close to that. I'm closer to moaning, like some shameless whore, and the more I do, the worse it gets.

I'm already wet, I know. I can feel my own slick cream every time I move, easing over my swollen clit and making all of those flushed folds so slippery, so ready to be parted and stroked, though I'm not ready for that just yet. I have to wait, until the pleasure reaches fever pitch. Until I'm gasping and tilting forwards towards the glass, pulling and plucking at my nipples while my face heats and my mouth makes this lewd sort of O.

Though even that isn't enough to push me over the edge. I'm close to doing it – hell, I've already traversed several of my own personal boundaries, like the noise-making and the voyeurism and the need to just take something, even if it makes me feel ashamed. But I'm not quite there, until he reaches a hand up, suddenly, in the light from the middle of The Courtyard and clear enough for me to see.

And then he does something I recognise immediately:

He strokes over the shape of my body, through the glass.

Of course I try to pretend otherwise at first. All the old issues take over, and I'm left imagining that he means something else. It can't be my body he's outlining, like that, so reverently, so slowly and softly. No one would want to touch me like that, and even if they did … that isn't my shape. That subtle curve at my hip, the fullness of my breasts … how can he even tell that I look like that beneath this shapeless gown?

And then I realise I'm practically clutching the thing to me, following the path he's making with that twisting, curving hand, and I know for sure. He's touching me, across a million miles of space and through two panes of glass. He's uncovering my body, those fingers finding their way over my jaw and my throat, clutching briefly in a way that thrills me, before sliding on down to other places I can't bear to touch.

Only I can, when he's touching them for me. He rubs his knuckles over my swollen mound and I find myself doing the same. I even turn my hand to get the exact same effect, pressing in when he does, forcing those knots of bone deep into my slick slit.

Everything parts easily for me, even through material. And my clit is so stiff and swollen that I barely have to push against myself to get some pressure on it. Just a little movement, a little rub back and forth, and I'm masturbating for a stranger.

A stranger who then makes a very specific sort of gesture, which I can't easily ignore or dismiss. *Lift your nightgown*, that gesture says. No more than a wave of his other hand, really, but enough to make me try. Quickly I do it, quickly, like some furtive flasher in a supermarket, aware of how easily I could be caught.

Someone could just slide open their curtain in the middle of the night, for example. Or maybe the girl from 9G will walk by, just as I had imagined. Just in time to see me expose my slippery pussy to this stranger's hungry gaze.

And it *will* look slippery, I know. I can feel the wetness on my perfectly waxed and oh-so-sensitive skin, and if I dared to glance down I know I'd see it glistening there. In fact, I don't even *need* to see it glistening there. It's obvious that I look as lewd and aroused as a woman could possibly be, because, after a moment of watching me, his hand goes to that place between his legs.

25

I can tell it does, even through all of this frustrating darkness. I can make out the motion of his thick bicep, as he works himself to the sight of me. And after a second of that desperate motion, he brings the fingers of his free hand to his lips and licks, then reaches forwards to stroke over my messy slit, through the glass.

He wants me to get off at the same time he does, I'm certain. He's going to jerk and come inside that clingy material, and when he does he wants me to do it, too. He wants me to slide two fingers through my swollen folds, find my clit, and stroke myself in time to the slow, easy rub he's giving himself.

And when he puts it like that, I find him impossible to resist. My face is flaming and my body is strung as taut as a wire, but I work my way through all of my mortifying slickness, until I've found that agonising point. That stiff little bud, so ready to be touched.

And then I just rub over it with the pad of my fingertip, just once, but once is enough. I can't even hold off long enough to see if I was right and that he's ready to come too. I just stumble over the edge into a thick, uncontrollable orgasm, more slipperiness spilling over my hand as I do, body spasming and twisting beneath the pressure of it.

I've never longed to know his name as hard as I do now, while calling out words that are not him. I moan *uuuh* and *God* and *yes*, but none of them fits my sultry stranger, my Serial Killer. They just have to make do as the most intense orgasm of my life barrels through my body, the sight of him stroking himself driving it on.

By the time he arches in his chair and shows me what he's been doing – hand sliding back and forth over his slick and very bare prick – I'm sure this thing has gone on forever. I'm still coming when he finally spurts, thick and copious and all over that neat little table of his.

Though that's not the best thing about it. No, the best thing about it comes after he's almost done. He sags back in his chair, and a split second before he does I see the side of his face – caught in pleasure and desire, as beautiful as it had seemed in the hallway.

And then I see his tongue, curling up to catch his upper lip – so greedily, I think, so different to the restrained person he usually appears to be – and that's all I need. That's what I take away from this lewd act, to store away for leaner, crueller times. Tomorrow I'll believe it was all just imagined desire and lust and loveliness.

And then I'll remember that tongue just kissing his upper lip, and make it real again.

Chapter Three

I'm aware that this is a ridiculous thing to do – like a stalker, rooting through things that belong to a person they're having a fake relationship with. But, after last night, I can't help it. I think of the name I couldn't call out and then I just wait, and watch which mailbox he goes to.

I do it surreptitiously, out of the corner of one eye.

And then once he's made his way past me – me with my back to him, him staring straight ahead, the air between us bristling like that moment just before lightning strikes – I go to the place he was. I run my fingers over the Sellotaped name on the front of that dingy grey metal.

Ivan. Ivan Orlinsky, it says, which of course only makes things worse. Now I'm thinking of far-off places in the past, where men with beards stride around through the snow and everyone has mysterious accents. He's the Russian of my imagination, the Polish of my dreams, or maybe some other nationality that I can't even think of.

Ivan Orlinsky, I think, from the land of TirAsleen. And then I have to stop, because the end of that tale is: who came across oceans of time to be with a tired, pathetic checkout girl called Abbie Gough.

It doesn't quite go, does it? Abbie and Ivan. Abbie is the girl you shove into the road on your way to a business meeting. She's not the mysterious sex partner of a dense-eyed man called Ivan.

And yet that's the name on the parcel he's left in my mailbox, in that same neat cursive script he used for the window. *Abbie*, it says, just above the impeccable seam he's made with the expensive wrapping – a perfectly straight and perpendicular join, held down by tape so crisply cut it could have been done with a machine.

Hell, maybe it was. It's called *him*. He's made of metal cogs and synchronised gears, and, when he's required to send an unexpected gift to a stunned girl, they perform the task with technical precision.

I can hardly bear to tear into the thing, it's that perfect. The paper's so thick, so glossy, it's actually nicer than most of the gifts I've ever received. It would be a shame to ruin it with rabid fumbling by my mailbox, as Mrs Hindleman from apartment 7F looks on.

So I take the gift upstairs. I sit on my bed and place it in my lap, for further inspection, though no amount of analysis will reveal his error. He hasn't made one. I have to somehow inch into this thing, with great and deliberate care.

Of course that only makes the anticipation greater. I can feel my eagerness clutching at my throat by the time I've tenderly undone the wrapping, and when I see the carved wooden box beneath my breath chokes off entirely.

He's made this box, I think. He's whittled it out of some dense, dark wood, for reasons I can't fathom. I just know they're there, these reasons, I know he's done this. I can tell by the way the box feels and looks, and, most of all, by how hard it is to get into.

He's made a puzzle box, seemingly equal on all sides, with no clear hinges or seams. It's just one endless whorl and curve carved into wood, as beautiful as anything I've seen. As disturbing, too. It's almost too intricate, I think, like a painting by that guy with the staircases – full of hidden thorns and secret upside-down passage-ways. If I touch the wrong thing, I'll be drawn into the labyrinth that lives at the centre of the underworld, and never escape.

Which is a silly thing to think by the light of *Wheel of Fortune*, blaring silently from my TV. But it lingers all the same, as I turn the box over and over, searching. There's got to be a way in, after all. He hasn't just carved me a block of wood, I'm sure – though in some ways it's still a surprise, when I find the key.

A little shock goes through me the moment I push against the body of a bird, wrapped all around in vines and leaves, and something that wasn't there before springs open. A little drawer, I think it is, but of course I don't dare look for the longest time. I glance up at *Wheel of Fortune* instead, and watch the colours whirl around.

And then when it seems like I care the least, when I'm barely paying attention, I slide the drawer out. I look inside the box he made for me, and find what's going to happen next in this brand-new life I've found myself in.

I'm going to wear a piece of jewellery, it seems. One he's made for me, as lovely as the box in its own way, but with a far different intent. The box is a beautiful puzzle, waiting for me to dare to open it. The gift inside is easy to read, immediately. I've seen similar things in dirty movies, though none quite as pretty as this. This is a work of art, really, as is the note he's printed on a piece of perfect cream card inside.

Wear it for me, the note says, though it's not the words I'm interested in. The words are a command, of the type men have given me all my life. But the question mark on the end ... the question mark is the thing I'm drawn to. I trace it with my fingers, that curve as compelling as the wood he's worked into such lovely shapes.

You can if you want to, that question mark says. *But*

not if you don't. And of course I already know what happens when I don't – he doesn't take all my privileges away from me. He won't hold my head under water until I pass out. It's not an ultimatum.

It's just a choice.

Yes, or no?

* * *

His gift takes some getting used to. It's easy enough to wear and fits me perfectly, as though that hand he ran over me through the glass was actually measuring the size of my hips. He made the gossamer strands with them in mind, and everything else followed: the trickling, teasing length of silver that slides between the cheeks of my arse and holds the base of the contraption tight to me. The V at the front that's almost like a pair of panties, until you get to the smooth rounded shape that now nestles between the lips of my pussy.

It's barely conspicuous when I look at myself in the mirror; I can't imagine what purpose it serves for my dark voyeur. But, oh boy, can I feel it. I can feel it when I walk and when I'm lying down. I can feel it as I sit behind my till at the Minimart, serving oblivious customers – that smooth plastic shape sliding over my clit at the oddest and most inconvenient times.

But most of all I can feel it after I've seen him in the

hallway, as composed and indifferent as he always seems in person. He could be carved in marble, as I walk past his implacable back. We could be total strangers who've never shared so much as a glance.

And then just as I'm at the height of this disappointment, just as I've convinced myself, again, that he doesn't care for me at all, a bolt of electric pleasure shoots from that little sliver of plastic, all the way through my over-sensitised clit and straight on down to the marrow of my bones.

I think I go down to one knee. I definitely stumble, at any rate. I know this because while I'm floundering in sudden stunned pleasure, he comes right up to me. *He comes right up to me* and then he *puts a hand on my elbow.*

And, as he does it, he says: 'Are you all right, Miss Gough? Here, let me help you up.'

As though I *simply slipped.*

Oh, let me process that for a while. Let me drown in it. That little slip of plastic between my legs ... it's not just a covering that quaintly teases. It's a *toy.* He's built some kind of little *buzzer* into the thing, and when I least expected it – when he seemed at his most casual and uncaring – he *purposefully activated it.*

And now he's helping me up in front of Mrs Belvedere from 8G, as though I had a funny and entirely spontaneous turn. It had nothing to do with him. He's an innocent passer-by, a good Samaritan.

Oh, and also, he's a *genius*.

I can hardly take him being this close to me, though naturally he knew I would feel this way. It was obvious that I'd be overwhelmed by his toy and then again by the clean, clear scent of him, like a forest in winter. And he knew that I'd bristle at the feel of his hand on my arm, pressing in a way that's somehow more intimate than that slippery plastic rubbing against my clit.

Though that's not really a surprise. Every part of my body is suddenly raw and exposed, a nerve ending he's stripped of all covering. He could touch me anywhere and I'd shudder to feel it, and I think he knows this.

Which is why he portions out his contact in increments, each one more exciting and certain than the last. A hand on my arm, a hand on my back – ever so light, as though he's not doing this at all. And when he finally steps away, his faint touch leaves me just as he knew it would: aching for more, but thrilling with the thought of what's to come.

Someday he'll actually kiss me, and I'll turn to dust and blow away.

'It's all right, Mrs Belvedere,' he says, but he doesn't look at her as he talks. He looks at me, eyes blazing with that odd sultry heat, and then he tells me: 'Abbie's fine.'

And it's true. I am.

Until he presses that damned buzzer again.

This time the sensation goes through me hard enough to force my teeth to clack together, though I'm glad they do. It stops the sound I want to make from coming out of me in a big glut, and saves me from further embarrassment courtesy of Mrs Belvedere.

She's staring at me oddly as it is, and, when Ivan says to her that I might need a lie down, her expression doesn't change. She's just waiting for the Serial Killer to do something odd and perverted, with devices and implements and other lurid things.

She doesn't know he already has. He's doing it right now as he guides me in the direction of the stairwell, that thing almost constantly humming against my clit. I've got absolutely no clue how he thinks I'm going to climb these steps with this hot pleasure washing through me, constantly, but he keeps going. He keeps urging me up the stairs. Pretty soon I'm going to orgasm, and then what?

I could barely stay on my feet the other night in front of the window. I can't keep putting one foot in front of the other like this, like nothing's happened. I have to cling onto the banister; I have to nearly crawl. And all the while he's walking behind me, pressing and pressing whatever sort of device he's using to drive me insane.

Which sounds weird enough on its own, until I realise how *slow* he must be walking to stay behind me. Like my dark and perverted shadow, just hovering at my edges.

Waiting for me to crack, I think. Waiting for me to turn desperately and beg him to stop.

Or maybe beg him for more. Because, dear God, I want to. I feel like I've been clinging to the outskirts of this pleasure forever, and, though I can climb the steps and keep myself steady and not give too many outward signs, inside I'm one long pulsing ache. My clit is close to throbbing, and I know without checking that my panties are soaked through.

I've wet myself because of a piece of jewellery, I think, and the shame that follows is …

Blissful.

I walk slanted down my hallway, one hand occasionally searching for the wall, and I don't care, I don't care. I'm lost in the heat that's engulfed my slippery pussy, and my usually so colourless face. I'm swaying down the tilted hallway in the labyrinthine box he made for me, drunk on desire and thick with sensation.

Sometimes the little toy buzzes fiercely, and my whole body jolts, primed. And then, just as I'm sure I'm about to burst into orgasm, it backs off to a low background hum, in a way that's far too practised. He knows what he's doing, I think, as he follows me to my door.

He's teasing me, ruthlessly, to the point where I can't even get my keys into the lock. I fumble with the bunch of them, fingers too frantic, mind reeling. He's going to come in, I think. He's going to follow me in and make me show him what I'm wearing, and afterwards he's going to get me to do things to him while he teases me into oblivion.

Like suck his cock, maybe, on my hands and knees.

In fact, the image is so strong – me straining for that thick, swollen head, hands fumbling over his strong thighs – that I almost go over at the thought. My clit spasms once, twice, and that tightly wound pleasure unravels. Just imagining his hand on the back of my head is enough … him guiding me, urging me on, the *smell* of him, the taste of his come flooding my mouth …

And then right in the middle of this delirious fantasy I make the fatal mistake of turning. Like Lot's wife, I think. Like a fool who doesn't know the rules of this game. Because, when I do, he's gone. The hallway is completely empty.

I don't even know when he left.

* * *

It's a test, I'm sure. A test of my resolve. He's given me a challenge, and now I have to see if I can stick to it. If I can hold out for this thing between my legs, instead of what I want to do – oh God, I want to rip it away. I've never wanted to masturbate so much in my entire life. Usually it's a stilted affair that I have to encourage and give permission for, maybe with a filthy movie or a smutty book. I can't have it unless something's persuaded me.

But this is the opposite. It's a denial, a restraint, and the moment said restraint is imposed I want to tear at it with my teeth. I don't need persuading to touch myself. I need persuading *not* to.

And he gives it to me. He gives, he gives, he gives, in a way I've never seen any man do. Sid would have bought me some underwear so *he* could look, and *he* could feel, but Ivan doesn't even ask me to strip. He just stands at his window and holds up the little remote, and when I press my face against the glass in desperation he lets me have what I need.

I feel it all the way over here, that sizzle against my oh-so-tender clit. And when I moan and press closer, when I writhe against the glass, he makes it go again and again and again.

I come within seconds. I come so hard I call his name, and other lewd things besides – like *yes* and *now* and *fuck me, oh please fuck me*. But of course he can't hear me. He can only see the disgusting things I'm doing, in place of all the things I want to say to him. I've got my fingers in my mouth as though they can somehow simulate his cock – in and out, as slow and steady as he's probably touching himself right now.

But when I open my eyes and dare to look, he isn't. He hasn't even taken his cock out, though I know how hard he is. I can see the thick and arousing shape he's made beneath the material, and I try to focus on that as he eases me through my stuttering, pulsing orgasm.

Just a hint of that hum, through the worst of it. And then a barely there ebb in the background, as I come to my senses. I'm not just fucking my own face with my fingers, I realise.

I'm rubbing myself against the glass, while I imagine him behind me. I've spread my legs and almost put my hand between, all pretence at propriety gone. Sid always had me in jumpers and jeans, whenever we went out. He always made sure I was carefully kept for him alone, pristine and perfect beneath the shapeless coverings.

But anyone could see me like this, and Ivan doesn't seem to care. As long as *I'm* enjoying myself, I think, and it's such a novel concept I could cry.

In fact, I do cry, when I realise he's not even halfway finished. Apparently one orgasm is not enough for him, and the buzz starts to cycle back up again. Slow at first, but then fiercer, more insistent, until I'm gasping again and completely outside my own boundaries. By the time I'm teetering on the edge of my second orgasm, I'm wondering what other filthy things I could get away with in front of the window.

Would I dare to fill myself with something, fuck myself properly in full view of him? I think I would, if only to get the message across to him more clearly: I want to feel you inside me. I want you to hold my hips and fuck into me hard, with this same cool glass pressed against my cheek.

I want everyone to know, I think, that I'm desperate to have you fuck me. And I don't care who disapproves of my desire, so much stronger and stranger than I ever thought it could be. I thought I'd died inside, I'm certain.

But as my clit swells against that maddening buzz, as my wetness runs down over my thighs and my back arches and I moan for him, oh God, I moan for him, I know I'm not dead at all. I'm alive, more alive than I've ever been, and it's at least in part because of him.

And I think he knows it. I think that's what he's aiming for, because, when I finally come around and gaze down at him through the glass, he doesn't look obsessed with his own pleasure or ready to take his turn.

His gaze is full of triumph, burning bright through that veil over his eyes.

Triumph, simply because he made someone else feel this good.

God, I want to tell him how weird and wonderful that really is.

Chapter Four

He's done something impossible, my Serial Killer, my Russian. He's made me want to go to him, even though I never thought I'd want to go to any man again. At night I still dream of Sid's hand fisting in my hair, of blood in my mouth and the redbrick house. I think of my shoes in a row and the lines of forbidden dust on things, and it seems insane.

But less so when he sends me another gift. Two gifts, when I'm used to none, and this one is a real doozy. It tells me everything I need to know, while simultaneously telling me nothing at all, and once I've finished with it this is how I feel:

Like my feet want to march to where he is sleeping. Like I don't care about keeping the glass between us, or the safe distance. The video tape strips all of that away, and leaves him as bare as I felt the other day.

It's labelled simply: surrender.

And when I see that one word on the strip of white I go numb all over. I think of what it could mean: *my* surrender, I'm sure. It could be a simple and stark demand for my submission, and so I put the tape into the player with shaking hands. He's going to ruin it now, I know.

Or I do until the screen flickers to life.

He looks even more handsome in this home movie than he does now. His hair is longer with a hint of curl, and the style gives his face a more tender feel. He's not as honed, either, not as *Patrick Bateman in his basement doing seven hundred crunches a day*, which I suppose helps to unwind me. In fact, it more than helps to unwind me – by the time the tape is thirty seconds in, my heart is already aching for him. I've clutched a hand to my chest, and I don't even know why.

He's probably going to bring a girl out, now, I think. And he'll make her crawl around on the floor like a dog. Then once he's done he'll look at the camera in this pointed sort of way, and I'll know.

That's the way things are supposed to be.

But that's not what happens. Instead, a man comes up on him from behind – a big man, a burly man, the kind of man who makes my stomach roll – and gets a hold of him by the hair.

He does it snake-quick and so roughly that I have to make a little sound. I can't help it. I can see Ivan's throat, beautifully curved and bared for the camera, as though the guy is going to put a razor to it.

And when he doesn't, I'm not relieved. My heart only rattles harder, higher, way up in my chest. It's practically beating in my throat, because of course I know what's coming next and, oh, I don't think I can watch.

What if he doesn't want to surrender, I think, even though I understand that this idea is impossible. The camera is dead on, precisely and carefully set up to capture a million details: the bulge of the man's massive tattooed arm, as he exerts some pressure. The gleam on both of their bodies. The slow close of Ivan's eyes, as the tension leaks out of his body.

This can't be an accident, or some silent witness to an assault. He's not even fighting this man, though I know he could if he wanted to. I can tell by the way he holds himself, muscles flexing so thickly beneath the skin.

And yet he doesn't use them. He barely struggles when the man forces him down over the table, that same table he sits in front of for me. He could have been doing this a year ago, when I first came here and didn't know his face. Maybe this man – this greedy, lusty-eyed man – lived in the apartment above me, and this was their ritual.

The man watched, and watched, and then one day it was just too much. He had to have my Ivan, and he does. He pins him down one-handed, while Ivan gasps soundlessly and squeezes his eyes tight shut, wanting this and not wanting it all at the same time, I'm sure.

And then the man simply spits between the cheeks of his arse, as rude as a raised finger at a garden party. Ruder, in fact. I clutch something else when he does it. I clutch between my legs.

Because if I don't I'm going to pass out. I'm already passing out. I'm watching my Serial Killer getting fondled and spread and stroked, right between the cheeks of his arse. He's even put the camera at such an angle that it can be seen clearly – that tightly clenched hole being slowly eased open by this fat-fingered man.

I can't breathe. I can't think. I'm sat right on the edge of oh-no-please-don't, with only the shameful *thud thud thud* between my legs to pull me back in. He meant this to be arousing, I know. I can tell he's watched it a thousand times by the crackles that flicker over the image and the general state of the tape.

And yet I hover between anxiety and pleasure. I lean forwards and draw back. What must it be like, to actually engineer such a scenario? To be so in control and so not at the same time? I suppose that's the appeal of it, really, though that isn't what I'm thinking when he finally forces a finger into Ivan's ass.

I'm not thinking of anything now. I watch him work Ivan open, slow and so deliberate. And of course I know he likes it, so really watching such a thing can't be anything *but* arousing. I mean, he enjoyed it the other night when I watched him do it to himself. So it's not such a big deal when I clutch at my swollen mound, like a reflex. Like I'm divorced from myself, the way he so clearly is ...

He doesn't have to think about anything either, I realise, and then I go ahead and do it for real. I slide my hand inside my panties, and find my stiff bud, too sensitive to touch directly but easy enough to circle.

While Ivan surrenders on-screen.

Go on, I think, go on, and the man does. He spits again so I can see it glistening between Ivan's arse cheeks, and, once everything's nice and wet, he works a second finger in, a third. Only this time I'm not on the edge of anything. I don't wince. I want him to go further, push harder, fuck him in a way that makes his hips jerk back and his body shudder.

And the man on-screen obeys.

He pumps him roughly, testing for a response. Waiting for Ivan to press his open mouth into the table and moan in a way I wish I could hear, before wrestling around inside his own grease-streaked jeans for his cock, flustered for the first time, it seems, and showing his overexcited true colours.

He wants to fuck him, badly. It's obvious. But it gets more so once he's freed his rigid prick. It's as hard and swollen as I've ever seen Ivan's, so slick and ready to fuck I'm uncertain for a second.

Was this really Ivan's idea? Or am I just imagining that because he *seems* like the puppet master? Maybe he's just *my* puppet master, and not this guy's.

Only then I see it. The guy hesitates, just as he's putting the condom on. His lips move around words that I have to rewind and see again. I have to fit the shapes his lips make to actual words, and on the third try I do.

You sure? The guy says, but of course Ivan isn't grateful for that. I wouldn't be either, if I'd orchestrated a dance and had to tell someone how to move halfway in. What would be the point, then? How would I find any relief in the charade, if it edged too much into fakery?

I couldn't.

And neither can he. His jaw clenches; he hisses a word. And, once he has, the guy just goes ahead and does it. Brutally. No holding back. One hand on Ivan's ass, that thick cock shoving in. I can't even imagine how it must feel, but I'm moaning and shivering in sympathy anyway.

The bliss on his face is enough to put me there. He looks like the weight of the world has been lifted off his shoulders briefly. He doesn't have to think – the way I don't have to think, once I'm aroused past the point of caring – he doesn't have to worry. Everything is designed and yet not, real and yet not.

And all of it centres around that slick, thick thing

fucking into him, that big beast over him, grunting and sweating and taking him to a place that I kind of want to go to, too. What must it be like to be so filled, to feel so used and yet know it's really you doing the using?

I can't imagine, but I do know this: he's close to coming before they've even really begun. His body is shuddering; his mouth is practically kissing the table. I can see the whites of his knuckles as he hangs on to its edges, through this impossibly hard fuck.

Because it *is* hard. Once the guy gets going, he doesn't hold back. He works up a lather, sliding that cock in and out of Ivan's ass. He does all of the things I would do if I were allowed to be so close to him: spreading everything wider, so he can watch his thick shaft filling that tight little hole. One hand running over Ivan's back, his arms, savouring every inch of him.

You're not going to get to do this twice, I think, and at the end of the tape I'm proved right. The guy fucks into him in a sudden frenzy, clearly coming hard and too quickly – the way I do a second later. My clit jerks against my pressing, sliding fingers, pleasure swamping me just as I see what Ivan has *definitely* re-watched a million times:

The guy ripping off the condom to spurt thickly all over that perfect golden back. He couldn't help himself, I think, and something about that is so viscerally exciting that I keep going, just as Ivan had forced me to the night before. I push one eager finger into my warm, wet hole, and then I stroke myself just beneath my clit. Just where it isn't too sensitive to take a second go.

And then I watch as Ivan stands up. He straightens, mechanically, as though sexual activity never took place.

Despite the fact that he's still hard. He's still hugely, massively hard, frustrated, too, by the look of him. His face is pink. There's an odd light in his eyes that's usually hidden by the veil. And when he hands the guy something – money, it's money – he shakes his head once.

No.

The guy asks again, and it's the same.

No. No more.

That's all you get with Ivan. One chance to give him the illusion he needs. Fail and you can never return, I guess, which is an awful theory to have in my head. I just don't know if I can give him this detached sort of passion forever, if I can be so far and yet so close. I'm already wanting to close the gap, and that urge gets stronger as I watch to the end of the tape.

I see my Serial Killer going about his business, putting his clothes back on. Ordering the table into the exact position it was in before, eyeing it this way and that until it's perfect.

And all the while I'm still masturbating. Even his meticulousness turns me on, it seems, though I know I'm about to give up by the time he comes to the camera. I don't want to get off like this, watching him slip back into his neat little shell. I don't want to do anything, anything at all.

And then he stares directly into the camera as he goes to turn it off. Those eyes of his like fire under water, burning through the lens and through his little routines and all the way over to me. They find me.

They *beg* me.

I know it then: this is what he wanted me to see. Not the fuck, the obvious organisation, his need to keep everything controlled and precise. It was that gaze he wanted me to see, and I do.

I see it as I roll into orgasm, with my hand still pressed against the screen.

* * *

I write the note a dozen times, then start again. And again. I waste a whole notepad, on words I can't say to him; I go through an entire box of cream cards I can't afford.

Nothing seems right. The device is too clumsy for someone like him. He needs a better key to fit his lock, as good as the one he used for me. A chance encounter, a beautiful gift, a question mark ... that's how he got me.

Only I don't know what his question mark *is*. I can't

fathom it out. I think he knows what happened to me – I can feel it in his deliberation and the slow patience of his approach. But what do I know about him? There are only clues: his rigid habits, his need to get fucked into oblivion. The sense of isolation that settles all around him, wherever he is or whatever he's doing.

I can't make out anything distinct from them. I can't even find out anything particular about him online, apart from: *Ivan Orlinsky obtained his Master's degree in computer science from Eldridge University. He is the owner and founder of Desinik.*

And that's it.

That's all.

Which is probably why I end up going with this for my first note. My first contact, through the glass, the gifts, the lens:

Tell me about yourself.

No question mark. At the very least I know this about him, after all: he doesn't crave choice as much as I do. He didn't crave a choice from that musclehead, and I don't think he's going to want it here.

Until I've posted the note and spent three days pacing my apartment ... and then I'm right back to having no idea. Maybe he absolutely loves choice. Who the fuck knows? He might like forcing a kangaroo up his left nostril – it's all Greek to me. I'm still in the beginner's pool of sexual ... *things*. I'm not ready for this level of emotional alienation and kinky tricks, and I know I should just tell him so.

Keep my curtains shut in the future.

Never speak of this again.

Never. Never. I swear it's going to be never. Better to have rarely loved and hardly lost, than ever to have loved at all. Better to be safe than sorry, better to stay out of the kitchen if you don't want to get burned. And I don't, so I promise this to myself. I promise that I'm going to end my weird association with Ivan right now.

Shame, really, that the toughest resolution of my entire life is so easily broken by a phone call. I pick up, expecting my manager from the store, and instead get this:

'What do you want to know?'

My heart stops. Mainly because it's forgotten how to go on beating. Of course I can't blame it under these conditions: I thought we were stalled at strange encounters through glass, and now he's calling me up. He doesn't even say hello or offer any kind of introduction.

It's just straight down to business.

Not that it bothers me. It doesn't even bother me that he sounds like an insurance salesman, following up on my query. In fact, that somehow makes this sweeter. More intense. His voice is so tightly drawn, so cool and collected, that all I can think is this:

Do I have the power to heat it up?

I guess in one way I already have. He doesn't strike

me as the type who gives words away freely, but he's giving them to me right at this moment. Now all I have to do is think about what I want him to tell me. What do I most want him to say?

The design company, I think, ask him about the graphic design company he owns. Keep things light, and then gradually work towards darker stuff. Find out about his hobbies, his favourite books. Tell him yours in return!

Oh, my mind is full of truly excellent ideas. My mind should go speed dating some time, and have fun conversations with bland people that the rest of me doesn't actually care about. While this rest of me asks Ivan the only thing I want to know.

'Was he your lover?'

I just blurt it out, breathlessly, running on instinct and adrenaline.

'That's a rather provincial question, don't you think?'

I barely even care about his response, because, oh God, I can hear he has an accent. I couldn't hear it before but I hear it now, buried beneath his words. He sounds almost American, until he gets to the ends of his sentences. Until his glassy tone rises, at the hint of a question mark.

And then I come back to reality, and focus on the words he actually used.

'Provincial?'

'Well, what you're really asking me is: am I gay?'

Shit. I didn't intend it that way at all. But when he

frames my question like that, that's how I sound. I'm a small-minded prude, shocked by his ability to take a cock up his ass.

'No.'

'Are you sure?'

'I wasn't ... I just ... I just wondered if you paid him at the end.'

'And that put you off?'

I can't even hate him for dogging me like this. He sounds too genuinely curious about someone as simple as me.

'No.'

'What could put you off then?' he asks, and I get that same feeling I got when I first saw the question mark, only stronger. He just seems so full of this odd sort of tease, suddenly, so eager to hear.

I didn't expect that. Aren't things supposed to be going the other way, into the land of closed-off-ness? He's meant to be as silent as the grave, maybe a little resentful that I made him call me up. Though really, when I think about it, I didn't force his hand.

He called me all on his own, and now he's asking me all on his own.

'I think you already know.'

He makes a little sighing sound, half contented, half not.

'Probably. But we're not talking about my keen powers

of observation now. We're talking about what you'd actually like to share.'

'Keen powers of observation? What do you mean by that?'

'I mean I took photos of you with a long-range lens and then made a giant shrine-like collage of your entire life.'

I think it says something about me that I believe him. I stare wide-eyed at nothing for a long moment, utterly paralysed.

Until he adds: 'I'm joking, Abbie. That was a joke.'

It's so hard to tell with him.

'I only use binoculars and a notepad.'

See? He's fucking stone cold deadpan. His pan is so dead he could lay it in a casket and bury it at Bellevue. They made a movie about him once: *Dawn of Ivan's Pan.*

'You birdwatched me?'

He laughs, and I swear to God my heart jumps in my chest. I didn't know he was capable of something as basic and human as laughter.

'I didn't really do that either.'

'Then what did you do?'

'I did this thing called seeing you around occasionally.'

By this point, he's so different to what I expected I hardly know how to get words out. I definitely don't know what I'm saying. Stuff just spills out of me in a rush, most of it blindly groping for the Ivan he really is.

'And that's all it takes? That's all it takes for you to … know things about me?'

He pauses then, and I find myself doing something very embarrassing. I'm straining, it seems, to hear every little detail of what he might be doing. It sounds like he's removing an item of clothing as he talks, clenching the phone between jaw and shoulder as he does so, but how can I be sure?

And more importantly:

Does this make me the same as him? Haven't I watched him, wheedled details out of him? Aren't I on the edge of my seat right now for more of this almost human contact? I am, I am, and yet …

Nothing can match what he then says to me.

'On Thursdays, you pick up dumplings from the Red Dragon. I know this, because you can never resist eating one before you get into the building. You walk by my window licking your fingers, or, if I'm really lucky, you're still eating one.

'You wear the same sorts of clothes no matter what the weather, come rain or shine, sleet or snow. Jumpers that trail over your hands as though you're afraid to let anyone know you have the ability to touch, take, hold. Skirts that graze the floor, because even that much would be too much, right, Abbie? Showing an ankle would be too much.

'You cut your own hair, because a salon would be vanity; you don't look anyone in the eyes, because that would be inviting someone in, wouldn't it? See, I know that last one because it's the way I am, too. Carefully judging people in tiny stages, through snatched glances … just waiting … waiting for someone to look up and make me look too.'

I think of that time in the hallway when we'd locked gazes. That feeling like a gun going off, like a hand squeezing in my chest. And then he speaks, and the gun goes off again.

'You know, nobody ever leaves their curtains open, except for you? I used to tell myself I wouldn't look, but sometimes I do. Just to see if you're looking, too.'

'I'm looking. I have looked, I mean. I did … before.'

Before I saw you touching yourself.

'Yeah? And what did you see?'

'I'm not as good at it as you are.'

'As good at what?'

'Seeing.'

He pauses then, but not for long.

'Give me your best guess.'

I swallow hard, thinking. I can't say *Serial Killer*, because that was Mrs Hoffman's term. It's not mine. Or at least, it's not mine anymore. I'm disowning it before it makes me feel any worse about all the assumptions I had, while he was busy admiring my dumpling eating from afar.

'You like routine, like me. Oranges on Thursdays. Mail at the same time every two days. I managed to see ...' I stop there, embarrassed. But he urges me to go on. 'I managed to run into you by working out when you'd be there, and being there too.'

Lord, how do I sound like more of a stalker than he does? My face heats just thinking of my little plots and schemes, of my dreams of seeing his amazing eyes and how many times I've played him helping me up in my head.

But I plunge on, regardless. If he can share, I can too.

'You wear the same outfit every day ... but more rigorously than I do.' The image of a dozen identical jackets swinging silently in his closet comes to me, and I voice it. 'I think you have several of the exact same uniform: the duffel coat, the leather boots, the white shirt underneath.'

There's a silence then, taut as a bowstring. And when he speaks again, his voice is rough.

'Very good. That's very good.'

'Is it?' I ask, because in truth he sounds more pissed than anything else. I've said the wrong thing, and now he's going to tell me off or hang up the phone – only he doesn't. I should have known; of course he doesn't.

'I've never known anyone remember so much about me. I'm not particularly memorable,' he says, and my response just jerks right out of me, too hot and too giddy.

'Are you kidding?' I ask, because seriously ... those *eyes* of his – almost navy blue and thick with feelings he won't tell you. Those cheekbones, that mouth like a kiss he's just waiting to give, his *manner* for God's sake. I don't understand anyone who wouldn't want to prise him open with a crowbar.

'What do you think is memorable about me, then, Abbie?'

I can't say the eye thing. Or the manner thing. And I'm definitely not going to say the thing that occurs to me a second after all that head-swooning over him: *Your cock, your incredible, delicious cock.*

Because that just sounds like I want to eat him. So I go with this, all tremulous and silly:

'Everything,' I say, only it doesn't seem like enough all on its own. There's no weight to *everything*, it doesn't mean anything on its own. But then again, nor does: 'I think you're so beautiful.'

Oh God. I'm getting into such a mess of emotion here. Whereas he ... he probably doesn't even know what emotion *is*. I'm wiping my feelings all over him, like a kid discovering finger painting for the first time.

'Despite the way I am?' he asks, after a moment, which at least mitigates that sense of making a mess on him. I mean, he clearly wants to know about this whole *beautiful* thing ... and I can let him know, too. I'm capable of clarifying.

'*Because* of the way you are.'

'And how am I, Abbie? Do you know? Have you figured me out?'

I think of the swinging jackets again. Of his boots, beneath, and of course I realise then what it reminds me of. It's how I used to have to do things, back at the redbrick house – as though there's some invisible presence always with him, constantly telling him to.

Though I don't say it.

'No.'

'I know why you are the way you are, Abbie. I know that you're scared, even now, that he'll find you.'

My stomach clenches, but it's not for myself this time. It's for him, and the invisible weight on his shoulders. What did someone do to him to make him this way? Who could have hurt him to the point where he still follows the same routine, without anyone there to impose the rules?

'I am,' I say, and then I gather the courage and just ask: 'Are you scared too?'

I'm afraid for the answer, though. I'm so afraid I'm squeezing my eyes tight shut, waiting for some horrible, inescapable sentence. It can't be just some person who abused him, I know. It's got to be something worse, something I can't even imagine.

'All the time.'

'Tell me what you're afraid of.'

'It doesn't have a name. It's just there; it's with me all the time. Feels like a big blackbird on your shoulders, doesn't it?'

Or an invisible hand, I think, but it's the same thing.

'Yes,' I say.

I'm crying. I'm crying.

'But you trust me when I say I can see things so clearly, right? You know I can see you?'

'Yes.'

'Then listen to me. Listen to me: the bird has gone now. It flew away when you weren't looking, I swear.' It's like he's reaching through the phone – just as he did through the glass – to stroke a hand over my back. 'Go to sleep now, Abbie. I'll go to sleep with you, and dream my blackbird is gone, too. You looked up at me, and it went away. For a little while, I swear, it went away.'

Chapter Five

I try the search terms 'Ivan Orlinsky' and 'murder', now that I'm not afraid to. But nothing comes up. His wife wasn't found floating in a pool of blood. He didn't kill his own son in a terrible car accident.

He's left no trace, like me. There's no sign of his blackbird, though I know it's there. I can tell it's there, because, when I go round to his apartment in a rush of fuck-knows-what, this is the response I get through the door:

'I can't come out now, Abbie.'

I feel like the biggest idiot on the planet for baking a goddamn pie. Apparently I know so little about intimacy I imagine it happens during a thirty-minute phone call. Now I'm just a fool stood on the wrong side of the door, holding baked goods. I don't even get a chance to say, *It's me, Abbie*. He probably saw me coming across the court-yard in a haze of adolescent love-feelings, and flipped his shit. He could probably tell it was me by the way I knocked – hell, who else is going to?

'I'm sorry, Abbie. I can't come out,' he says again, while I struggle around in this mire of uncertainty. What does he mean, exactly, by 'can't come out'? He doesn't even know that's what I want. Maybe I just want to go in, though I don't see how that would be any less prob-lematic here.

It's pretty clear. It's not that he can't come out. It's that he can't even open the door. He's forgotten how, because of that time thugs broke in and almost beat him to death. Or did he once answer the door to a real serial killer, and this is the result? The frustrated sound of his voice, the dull thud of his body against the wood.

He wants to, I think. He just can't.

Though I can't help remembering that he did for some burly guy he paid. He let him, all right. Why not me? I probably said too much, seemed too needy. After all, he's technically a stranger, and I started crying on the phone.

I've probably got attachment syndrome, to match his detached version of the same thing. We're so fucked up we could convince Freud to analyse us from beyond the grave. I'm sure he'd have lots of undead things to say about the barriers we've built up, the things we can't say, the fact that I'm actually ludicrously excited when he calls me later on.

Despite the way he starts the conversation.

'That was fucked up, right?'

He sounds as certain as I am.

'I don't know. I probably would have done the same thing,' I say, but I'm lying. I've got the image of him coming to my door in my head, right now. I'd open it and glue my body to his, let him lift me off the ground. Kiss him, kiss him, kiss him. I can even see the clothes we would be wearing in this imaginary fantasyland: me in something less baggy and formless, something pale blue and clingy so I can see the shape of our bodies sandwiched together; him without that coat. Barely anything between us.

'So you don't trust me.'

'You started this. I should ask you first – don't *you* trust *me*?'

'It's not about trust.'

'Then what?' I ask, but I think I already know. *Contact*, I think it is. *Intimacy*. He can meet me in the hall, touch my elbow. Help me up. He can talk to me on the phone or send me gifts that drive me nuts. But he can't accept that image I've got in my head:

My body with his body. No spaces between us.

'Are you thinking about what the *what* might be?' he asks, and I kind of hate how amused he sounds, how

63

sure. I was so fucking hurt that he didn't open the door. Does he know how much it cost me to go over there and do that?

'I'm thinking about what an asshole you are,' I say, and it's only afterwards I realise what I've done. I haven't spoken to anyone that way in *five years*. In fact, I don't know if I've *ever* spoken that way to anyone. It makes my cheeks flame immediately and the urge to be sorry rises up inside my throat, like a sickness. He's going to kill me now. He's going to backhand me across the face, through the phone.

It almost makes me jump out of my skin when he laughs instead.

'I know. I know I am. I'm sorry, Abbie.'

Oh God – *accountability*. Is there anything sexier on a man? Actual *apologies*. I could drown in him, I could.

'If it's any consolation, you came real close to making me open up.'

'How close?'

'A hair's breadth away. A heartbeat away.'

I can hear his accent again, thick and sticky.

'And what would have happened then? If you had let me in?'

'Are you sure you want to know?'

'I do.'

He pauses then, the longest pause of my life. But he makes up for it when he finally, finally speaks.

'I would have run my hands all over your body. You know how hard it was to keep them off you on those stairs? When you could hardly walk? Every time I didn't touch you, it made me ache.'

Of course I automatically think of what he would have found if he'd given in and done it. All the lumps and bumps all over me ... all those vast expanses of pale, pasty skin ...

'You don't even know what I look like under my clothes, not really. You –'

'That just makes it sweeter. I spend long nights imagining your shape under those shapeless things. Imagining my hands pulling the material taut around the curve of your hip, the roundness of your breasts. Would you let me do something like that, Abbie?'

'Yes. Yes. Anything.'

'Would you let me pull it over your head?'

'Oh God, yes, take it off me. Take everything off.'

He makes a restless sound that I appreciate ten times more from him than any other man. He's so closed off he can't even open his front door, but, oh, he can sigh for me. He can say: 'Fast, or slow?'

'You decide,' I say, and for once in my life it's good to do it. Yeah, he can decide. That's OK, it's OK. I know he's not going to tell me to do anything bad.

'Slow,' he says. 'Slow.'

And, oohhhhh, that's not bad at all. I'm dying; I'm

dead. I'm hunched over the phone like a starving animal, guarding my stash. The receiver has turned to a hot, slick mess in my hand, and I'm just barely hanging onto it. I'm clenching the plastic tight, but it's not going well.

'Lift that jumper over your head. Go on, lift it now for me,' he says, so I do.

I fumble my way out of it then discard it on the bed. Now I'm only in my bra, my big ridiculous skirt.

'I'd get my hands underneath that jumper and just slide it over your head. Take my time working through the layers, unravelling you. You wearing a bra?'

'Yes.'

'I'd like to keep that on, at first, just peel the cups away from your breasts. See you like that, with the straps still framing those gorgeous curves. Because they are gorgeous, right, Abbie?'

'I don't know. I don't know,' I say, but only because anything more seems impossible. I'm almost struck dumb by his ability to say all of these amazing words once we're not actually looking at each other. Once I'm not lurking on the other side of his door, like some strange new sort of threat.

Girl with a pie, I'll call it. It's almost like *guy with an axe*, if you squint hard enough.

'You do know. Go to the mirror and do what I've just described, then tell me exactly what you look like.'

I could go to the window, I almost say, but it's like

him with the door. Too much, too much, and besides ... I'm not sure that's the point. He doesn't want to look at me. He wants me to look at myself, which doesn't seem quite as hard.

Until I do, and then it's very hard indeed. I look clumsy, I think – silly pink bra caging my breasts in, the waist-band of my big skirt over my belly – and I tell him so.

But he won't have it.

'Are you sure?' he asks, then more, more, oh unbear-ably *more*. 'I know what your skin looks like ... lumi-nescent, like cream. And those beautiful breasts ... they tilt up a little, don't they? Full and heavy but with just that little tilt, made near obscene by the straps now around them. Am I right?'

He's right about the obscene part. My nipples are so stiff they look sore, all red and spiky and rude. And the straps on either side are just ever so slightly cutting in, like some strange sort of bondage that I'm not quite familiar with.

'I bet they're almost begging to be touched, right now,' he says, and he's not wrong. There's a hollow ache thrumming through my body, and it starts at those stiff points and ends between my legs. *Touch yourself*, it says, *go on*, but I can't quite make it happen until he tells me.

'Go on,' he says, as though he knows. He knows I find it hard and wants to make it so easy, and it is, with him talking in my ear. He lets me know all the things I wasn't sure about, like how lovely I must look and how good it must feel to just run a hand over the smooth slope of my breast. I don't even feel bad about the little gasp I let out when my palm grazes over my stiff nipple.

Because he's there to suggest otherwise.

'Oh yeah, baby. Tell me how it feels,' he says, so I do.

'Soft. Really soft … and my nipples are tight.'

'How does it feel when you touch them?'

'Like this,' I tell him. 'Like this.'

And then I moan, just for him. I've never moaned for anyone before. My life is a ruin of fake sighs and phony *yeahs*. But he pushes me to some real point of arousal without even trying, without even touching me, and I can't help being grateful for that.

I show him my gratitude, with words I could never previously say.

'Every time I touch them this bloom of pleasures shoves down between my legs, close to an orgasm. Really close. I can hardly stand up for it, but I don't want to sit down.'

'You want to stay and look at yourself.'

'Yes. Yes.'

'Are you beautiful, Abbie?'

'I seem beautiful when you talk. Oh *God*, that feels good.'

'What does? My words, or the way you're touching yourself?'

'Both. All of it. Everything,' I say, though I'm only partially telling the truth. His words are amazing and the way I'm plucking at my tight nipples feels good, but there's so much more I desperately want.

If he could just tell me it's OK ...

Or if I could just tell him. I can. I will. I'm going to.

'I want to lick my fingers.'

'Why?' he asks me, but his voice is very hoarse now. I think he knows. I think he more than knows, in fact – I think he might be touching himself, as I moan and whisper into the phone.

'So that I can rub that slickness over my stiff little nipples. It's not enough, like this. But if I just put my fingers in my mouth and suck ...'

'Ohhhh yeah. God, yeah. When you did that for me in front of the window, I almost lost my mind,' he says, but all I can think of is how still he had seemed. Fierce in the eyes, but motionless otherwise. You would never have known that he was close to losing his mind, but then, that's the benefit of words. That's the benefit of being just this little bit closer.

Now all I have to do is get him to come closer still.

'You liked that, huh? I do too. I like imagining it's you when I slide them into my mouth. My fingers aren't as thick, of course, but I can almost feel it.'

'You can feel my cock in your mouth?'

'Yes. Mmmm, yes. Do you want that?' I ask, but he

doesn't answer me directly. Not yet anyway. A little bit more maybe.

'I want you to make your nipples all nice and slick. Do that for me, Abbie. Rub that wetness all over them, and tell me how it feels.'

I'd be frustrated by his evasion if I didn't love how much he wants to know about me and my responses. Not his. *Mine*. My pleasure, my desire, the things that turn *me* on. I swear this wouldn't be half as easy as it is if I didn't feel so *valued*.

'Like I could come just from touching them,' I say, and this time I get a full throated groan from him, so loud I almost sink under the pressure of it. The sigh was enough on its own to waste me, this is beyond what I thought I'd get.

And he's definitely masturbating as he gives me it, too. I can hear the slick shuttle of his hand on his dick, quick enough to make him nuts but not quite enough to make him come. He's waiting for me, I think, before he goes over. He's waiting to get his composure back so that he can say to me: 'No. No, not yet. Take your skirt off first.'

But I'm like him. I can hardly do anything. I can hardly think the way I normally would; I'm half insane with arousal. My pussy is one thick throb between my legs, and when I shift I can feel every little inch of it – my swollen clit, my slippery folds.

Taking off an item of clothing is agony, on my already oversensitised body. Just the feel of the material sliding over my legs is enough to make me sob, and, of course, it's all so difficult. It's nearly impossible. My feet get tangled in the masses of material and all the while I can hear him breathing too hard and being too expressive.

He's not like this, he's not like this, I think. But apparently he is once he's worked himself up to a certain point. He's like me in that regard, exactly like me – one half cut from the same cloth I'm made out of.

And, ohhh, that's even better than all of this blistering, impossible sex.

'Are you naked?' he asks me, and I tell him I am aside from the bra. I can see my sex glistening beneath the tiny strip of hair I've got, clit so swollen it's visible between those flushed folds, and somehow I tell him that, too.

And he answers in the best possible way he could.

'Oh God, baby, I want you. I want you.'

'You want me?' I ask, because I need to hear it again, before the door slams shut. I'm talking to him through a crack in it, and one of his hands is almost all the way through to me.

But the chain's still on.

'You've no idea how much I want you. I want to bury my face between those legs, taste how wet you are, lick that stiff little clit.'

71

'Ohhh, it's so stiff. I can hardly touch it.'

'I'll touch it. Spread your legs for me, baby,' he says, and now I can no longer tell. Who are these words persuading – him or me? Am I at the door, gazing through at him?

I feel like I am, but, if so, he should know:

It's open. I'm open. At last, I'm open.

'Anything,' I say to him. 'Anything for you.'

And I mean it, too. I spread my legs in front of the mirror, and tell him how it looks when he asks – so slippery I can hardly stand it, so flushed with arousal and ready to be fucked.

'You want to fuck me, Ivan?' I ask, and I do it just as I ease one finger into my warm, wet hole, imagining it's him. Imagining it's him with his face between my legs, just like he said, and those good, thick fingers fondling me, stroking me, pumping into me steady and slow.

And then after a while he wouldn't be able to stand it – I can tell he wouldn't. He's groaning almost constantly now, and it makes the image very easy to see. Him moving over me, that big thick cock seeking out my entrance.

I can almost feel it … ohhh God, I can, I can. I'm almost there, with him over me and my hands between my legs and the sound of his voice as he says it, just for me. That one thing I wanted to hear more than any other thing in the world, so sweet in my ear, as I slide down, down into orgasm.

'There's nothing I want more. Ohhhh, Abbie, my Abbie. There's nothing I want more.'

Chapter Six

We do the same thing every night for a week from that point on. He calls me, and sometimes we talk idly about this or that. He likes Russian poets, and tells me so in dream-like detail, while my head fills up with snow-covered landscapes and curling spires. He says, *If I do not see you, I feel: minutes, as centuries, are endless,* and then again when I ask him to speak the words in Russian.

Though it's better in the latter. It's like hearing his real voice, his secret voice, buried beneath a life mostly lived in America. *When did you leave?* I ask him, and he tells me in those same clotted-cream words, those foreign words that I have to look up later on.

He was four apparently. Four years old and thirty-five now, but his Russian still sounds as foreign and foggy to me as anything I've heard in old spy movies. It sounds thicker than that, in fact, guttural almost, and when he speaks it I can't help putting a hand between my legs.

'Say it again,' I tell him, and he laughs and asks me if I'm really masturbating to the sound of his voice. As though it's crazy to get off on that sultry, smoky sound.

Christ, even his English is sexy, and I tell him so.

'No matter what language you're using your voice drives me crazy.'

'Really? I always thought I sounded cold.'

'No.'

'Mechanical.'

'Oh God, oh God ... keep talking.'

He laughs, a sound I'm getting used to hearing.

'Now you're just teasing me,' he says, and I wish I could tell him I was. But he got me worked up with the poetry and now he's being all amused and surprised ... what does he want me to do? I'm still wet from the ham salad sandwich discussion we had the other day.

He likes sliced cucumber. I do not.

I get turned on over conversations about food.

Whereas he ...

'Are you really touching yourself?'

'Yes.'

'Where?'

'I've just got my hand a little way inside my panties. Just rubbing over the lips, there. They're all slippery already, hearing you talk,' I say, because he doesn't really have to persuade me anymore. There's no moment when I pause, nervous and afraid of what he'll think.

He's so withdrawn that I just need him to know before he pulls away any further. I want to go to him, for all the ways he can't come to me – and then he does, he does.

'I've got my hand on myself, too,' he says, while I thrill over this small victory. Usually it's all me: *what am I doing, what do I want to do*? It's almost a novelty to have to switch it around on a man. Put the focus back on him, and wait for him to share.

In fact, it's more than a novelty, more than a thrill.

It's a huge fucking turn-on.

'You have?'

'I always do when I talk to you.'

'Oh that's good. Tell me how it feels,' I say, because, hey, I learned from the best. If he can coax it out of me, I can coax it out of him.

'Ready to burst. Hard enough to ache.'

'But you're not stroking yourself?'

'Not yet. I like to wait.'

'Until what?' I ask, though I think I know what he's going to say. He's both unreadable and utterly easy, at the same time – like he really is a half of me. Sometimes I'm so certain what I'm going to do, and other times my will likes to turn on me, needle me, make me do things I didn't know I wanted.

Is this what he wanted to do?

'Until I hear you coming, too. You like the sound of my voice when I talk, I like the sound of yours when you come – those moans you make, the sense of abandonment. It's like a promise of something I could do if I really wanted to.'

'You could moan for me like that?'

'Is that what you want?' he asks, but, ohhhh, that's a dangerous question to pose. He's got to know what the answer is by now, because I'm sure I've said it to him a dozen times. We took a bath in our respective tubs together the other day, and I said it to him then. I said it to him as he urged me to use the spray from the shower head on my eager clit, and I said it to him again after he sent me a rather hard and thick sort of gift.

The one I grab now, in lieu of the one thing he won't give me.

'I want you to fuck me. I want to feel you inside me,' I say, just as I slide his perfect present through my slick folds. It's carved wood – just like the box – so of course the whorls and curves feel just incredible against my clit.

But there's only one thing I really have in mind.

'You know I want that too.'

'How much?'

'So much that I'm picturing it now, as I slide my hand over my cock. I'm so stiff and swollen I'm sure I'd hurt you. I'd have to lick that sweet pussy first.'

'God, Ivan. Oh God, yeah, fill me with that big dick.'

'Work you open with my fingers, get you nice and wet. Are you wet for me now?'

'I'm so wet I can just take that gift you sent me ... Oh yeah, feels so good sliding inside me. Is that what you'd feel like? It's so hard and thick.'

'You know what I'd feel like. You've seen me.'

'Yeah. Ohhh yeah, you're so big.'

'Is that good? Is that good going in? Fuck yourself with it, baby. I want to hear you come on that thing. I want to hear you take it and take it.'

'I am, I am. I'm fucking myself so hard. Just the way I want you to.'

'You want me to get you on your hands and knees?'

'Fuck, yes.'

'You want me to pound into you, make you come, make you scream?'

'Please. Just come to me, come to me,' I say, but he won't give in. He tells me things he knows I want to hear instead – like how hard he's jerking himself and how close he is to coming. *I'm gonna spurt all over myself*, he tells me, in such a filthy, half-groaning tone of voice that it couldn't be more obvious what he's trying to do.

'I know you're trying to change the subject,' I say, and now his groans are more frustrated – with himself, or otherwise.

'Really? I thought it was called *having an orgasm*. I guess my English has slipped since meeting you.'

'You're not going to have an orgasm. You never come this fast.'

'Maybe it's the thought of fucking you.'

'Why think when you can have the real thing? I'm so ready, so hot and wet and tight. Don't you want to feel that? Don't you want to feel me around you?'

He moans, then, and contrary to what I've just said I can hear him going over. He always makes the same sound when he does – rough and guttural, not quite in control of himself. And I can hear how frantic he's being, how hard he's fucking himself.

He likes a tight hand on his cock, I know, and when he's climaxing it's almost as though he's punishing himself. He's punishing himself for wanting this, the way Sid used to punish me – which is when I realise. It's not an invisible hand he's got, hovering over him. It's his own hand. It's his own hand, holding him back.

And when it slackens, just a little, oh, it's like the sun coming out in the middle of winter. It's the first time I've ever orgasmed to words that are barely sexy at all.

'Tomorrow, I promise,' he says, and in answer I come, and come, and come.

Chapter Seven

He's a liar, though. He's a filthy liar, leading me on. I thought he meant that tomorrow would bring him, at my door. But instead there's another gift, which I can't quite bring myself to like. I can't bring myself to like it until I open it, and after I have I feel bad for ever doubting him. How could I have thought he wouldn't keep his promise? He's done nothing but be absolutely and intensely honest with me about everything, from how hot he likes his baths to what brand of mayonnaise he likes on his sandwiches.

And if there's one big thing he's kind of holding back, well, that's OK. At least he gives me his word, and holds to that. He holds to it after half an hour of mystery and me wondering what on earth this thing is.

It's a box like before. This one is smooth, corner-less, white, though I get the impression he made this one too, somehow. He melted it and moulded it until he came up with something just as initially frustrating, and just as magical when I finally understand.

It's not as obvious as the toy he sent me, in one way, because with that I knew what he wanted me to do. I knew he wanted me to wear it and walk around as though nothing was happening, my arousal a secret only I could know. But although the function of *this* item is clear, the meaning is not.

It's just a blindfold. What does a blindfold have to do with his promise? He didn't say, *Tomorrow, I'll send you something to cover your eyes.* He said, *Tomorrow I'll be with you.* I mean, that was what he meant, wasn't it? I've spent all day in that wretched store, wriggling on the spot, in anticipation of what might be waiting for me.

This just doesn't seem right at all.

And then I see the key. I see the note, in his curlicue handwriting, like Cyrillic script without the Russian.

Let yourself in. Wear my gift. Wait for me.

I can only come to one conclusion. And the conclusion turns me into a giddy, trembling wreck. My heart tries to escape out of my chest, then settles down, then goes for the exit all over again. For five long minutes, I don't know what to do with myself, and it doesn't get any better when I reread the note and fully consider what it means.

He wants me to go to his apartment. He wants me to go *inside* his apartment – maybe when he's not there. After all, he's left me a key. That implies he won't be around when I let myself in to what has now become a mystical cave of wonders in my head.

I'll get to see the table, and the carpet that I vaguely remember as a kind of rough green pile. There's a kitchen just off his bedroom-slash-living-room, and now I'll get to do more than just kind of see it from afar on a crackling video tape. I'll get to explore it, as though somehow it's going to be way, way different to mine.

Even though I know it won't be. Everything's the same in The Courtyard.

It just doesn't feel it when it's him.

That's why I'm shaking, before I've even gotten to his door. I've got the gift clutched in my hand, half of me unsure of what the instructions were now. Did he say wear it first, and then go in? And, if he did, how on earth am I supposed to fit the key in the lock? I'll still be stood here when he returns, hands fondling all over the goddamn door for the keyhole.

Which decides it for me. I have to go in, and *then* wear this strip of red lace, despite how achingly intrusive that seems. It's like breaking the seal on an airtight bag. I open the door and almost hear something hissing or shushing, and then the undisturbed air of his apartment rushes against my face.

Everything is so still, inside. So quiet. And I was right, too, to imagine his apartment would be different, because somehow it is. Things look more polished in here than they do in mine. The walls almost have a reflective surface; the fixtures and fittings are so smooth and modern. My lights are held up by these old crooked brass sorts of things; his look near futuristic.

The kitchen's the same, too. I hardly dare to go in it, but, once I'm sure he's not here, I take a little step through the door. I take in the white and black checked flooring, which puts my own peeling linoleum to shame. The double-wide refrigerator, steel grey and shining, and the sink to match.

In fact, everything matches. Everything is neat and ordered and perfect. The bank of computers he's got against one wall hum in this low, comforting sort of way, as though to say they'll always be there and always be working, because Ivan takes such good care of them. He takes care of the single plant he's got, of the clothes that hang in his closet, just like I thought. And lastly, the thing my eyes want to settle on after everything else has been thoroughly examined:

His bed.

It shouldn't look inviting, but it does. Those crisp cool sheets, pulled hotel-room taut. The neat fold-down he's done, as though this really is the Hilton instead of his home. Even the pillows are somehow wrinkle free, plumped and smoothed to perfection.

I don't know whether to be unnerved, or oddly thrilled. I've never seen a man do this sort of thing for himself. I didn't know a man was capable of living like this, unless he'd ordered and bullied and beat a woman until she did it for him.

But not Ivan. He's got his own demons driving him to this, and that thought takes away any pleasure I found in his care and precision. He doesn't delight in this, I'm sure. He's just waiting to stop, he's wanting to stop, and maybe this is what I am to him.

I'm messing things up.

His choice of someone like me says it all, really – my big, crazy hair and my sloppy clothes and my eating of things with my fingers. The other day he asked me to describe my bed to him, and when I told him – *like a shipwreck, like a bomb's hit it, like I've been fucked for five days in the sheets* – he sighed this contented sigh and asked me to tell him again.

It hadn't made much sense at the time, but I think it does now.

The very thing Sid hated about me, Ivan craves. He wants disorder in his strictly ordered life, and I can give that to him. I can. But first I've got to sit on the edge of his bed with this blindfold on, and that's a much taller order than I thought it would be.

The material's heavier than it had seemed in the box, once I've tied it around my head. I can't even open my eyes behind it, and for a long panicked moment I consider loosening the knot I've made. If I get it just right, I could possibly see through the red lace, just a little. After all, I could see my palms through the material when I held it in my hands. It's not dense and impenetrable.

But somehow I don't. I leave the blindfold as it is, and try my best to be patient. To be calm. He'll come in and everything will be fine, because I trust him. I do.

So why do I freeze when I hear him walk into the room? Hell, I freeze when I hear his door go, though after a moment I understand why. It's not really because of him at all. It's because of the sudden and sharp idea that comes to me while listening blindly for the turn of the doorknob, the sound of the door shutting, the heavy thud thud of someone's shoes on the carpet.

This could be anyone. Maybe it's the intruder I made up in my head to explain why he is the way he is. Maybe it's that big guy, and actually this scenario really is all Ivan – he hired that musclehead again, to give me the going over he can't.

Oh God. Oh God, that last one sounds much more plausible than I'd like it to be. I mean, what do I really know about Ivan, aside from stuff about sandwiches? Why do I trust him so closely? I never thought I'd trust anyone again, and yet here I am with a blindfold on, in a strange man's apartment, just because we ate dinner together the other day, through the phone.

I'm crazy, I think, and the second I feel his breath ghosting against my cheek, his presence bristling so close to me, I show it. I shove back on the bed, hands scrabbling for purchase. Legs almost kicking out against the sheets, some awful sound in my throat.

'No,' I tell him, and then even more childishly: 'No, I don't like it.'

But I can't make the right moves to rectify the situation. I can't get the blindfold off, because I'm an idiot who tied it too tightly. Now it's like a noose around my throat, trapping me in some deadly scenario with a filthy, boorish stranger.

'Abbie.Abbie,' he says, and it's his voice, but I still can't. I need to get away, I need to rip this lace off, and I continue to need all of these things until he grabs a hold of my flailing hands and puts them on his face.

'It's me, Abbie. Here, here,' he says, but he doesn't need to. The second he offers me such an intimate thing, all the panic drains out of me. My shoulders drop; I stop the kicking. I stop and just feel that face I've seen a thousand times in my dreams. In the hallways of this stifling place.

He's just as beautiful as he seemed, when I could see him with my eyes. More so, in fact, because my fingers pick up a million things I'd missed – like how smooth his skin is, in all the places where there isn't any stubble. He has a slight cleft in his chin that I didn't notice before, and his jaw feels squarer than it looked through the window. Heavier.

I thought his face was quite narrow, but it isn't.

And, oh, his mouth. I run my thumb over his upper lip, and feel out that soft Cupid's bow shape, so sweet I could mistake it for a woman's if it were not for the bristle of his stubble all the way around. The contrast is delicious, electric, and before I know what I'm doing I'm making a meal of it.

I'm practically fondling his mouth, fingertips tracing the shape. Thumb almost daring to go in, but not quite, not quite. I can't do something like that, while I'm still pretending I'm panicked and in need of the reassurance of his face.

No, no.

I have to wait, *until he goes ahead and does it for me*. He turns his head and presses into my touch, first with his face in a way that makes me sigh – like an animal seeking heat, I think, like a beast rubbing its fur against my palm – and then with his mouth.

He kisses me. He kisses my fingers, makes them wet. And just when I'm tense all over, waiting for more ... he takes one into his mouth, just like we talked about. He licks the length of one finger, and I feel what I've only dreamed about for days, and days and weeks.

The warmth of his lips, his kiss ... the feel of him actually touching me. It's crazy how intense that build-up makes such a simple thing. It's like he's created a new erogenous zone in the webbing between my fore and middle finger. It's like that place has a direct line to my clit, and every flicker of his tongue resonates through it.

God knows what's going to happen if he progresses to anything lewder. I might pass out from the pleasure, because Lord knows I'm almost doing that very thing now. I'm shaking by the time he's done. I'm shivering all over, and half terrified of the feel of him, moving on to some place new.

He kisses the inside of my wrist, and that's too much. Everything is heightened to a perilous degree, not just by that long slow climb into real live touching, but by the blindfold, too. I can't see where he's going to go or what he's going to do, which probably explains the little gasp I give out when he puts an actual hand on my arm.

That's him, touching me. Only he's not just touching. He's grabbing, I know, and pulling me down, down into what is obviously going to be a kiss. Oh God, he's going to kiss me, or maybe I'm going to kiss him, because once I'm halfway there I forget every fear I ever had and just sink into this thing I've wanted for so long.

Of course, I realise then that I never thought I'd get it. I didn't think I'd get to put my hand in his hair, shaky but sure. I didn't think I'd feel him sliding his own hand up through *my* hair, like a mirror of my touch.

Or the climax of some Hollywood movie.

And then his mouth touches mine all tentative and tender, and I could drown in it. He doesn't kiss me, he feels me out, searching for that rhythm I like best before falling into it. His mouth slants against mine, not quite open at first but then, oh then ... I feel him give himself over to it. He catches my upper lip between his, draws the movement out as slow as syrup ...

Before going back for more.

It's the best and worst kiss of my life. The best because of how new it feels, like I've never done this before and every move I make could be wrong, or right. Everything is startling, everything is fresh, and I'm trembling with it. I'm almost sliding off the bed, because most of my muscles don't want to hold me up.

But there's a worst part to this, too, and it comes about five minutes in. It comes when I actually realise that we've been making out for *that* length of time, without going any further. He's not got his hand up my skirt and I'm not groping under his clothes for that incredible body.

We're just doing this, like two teenagers starved of contact. It's no wonder it feels like the first time – we're only doing what first-timers do. He isn't even using any tongue, until I realise how slow this is all going and how desperate I am for more and, ohhh, I don't mean to.

I just do. I use that sudden lack of muscle mass to just ease myself off the bed, and then once I'm in his lap I get my arms around his neck. I press my body to his, in that way I'd imagined doing.

But, most importantly, I kiss him like I'm never going to get to do it again. I cram every little part of him into my memory: the taste of his mouth, like mint and like that wintry smell. And I get great handfuls of his short dark hair, burrowing through to the root. It's so soft, softer than it looks, though his hair is not the thing I'm concentrating on.

I focus on the feel of his mouth, wet and hot and suddenly really open. Most of me is sure that he's going to back off at any second, that he'll find this too much or too clumsy. But it's not like that at all. It's like I thought before instead ... about the mess that he secretly wants.

The greedier I am, the sloppier I am, the more he seems to enjoy it. I devour his mouth whole and he groans for me, and when I just let my tongue flicker into his mouth – just a little – the groan gets louder. I feel it vibrate on down through my body, before finally pooling between my legs.

Where everything is far too hot and far too wet. I think my pussy's been replaced by a great throbbing fist, and I know I've soaked through my panties. We're just kissing, but I've soaked through my panties. I'm groaning and wriggling, and of course I only get more shameless when I feel his hand on my back.

And then my ass.

He makes the move slowly, like maybe he's thinking I'll say no halfway there. But once he's got a handful of me he gets bolder. His other hand joins the first, and suddenly I'm lifted off my knees.

He actually *lifts* me. All I can do is hang on tightly and kiss him harder, because, good God, I don't think anyone's lifted me before in my entire life. He even stands with me clinging to him like some sort of sex-crazed monkey, legs wrapped tight around his waist, arms around his neck.

He has to practically prise me off him, just to get me spread out over his bed, and even then I seem to have a complete absence of shame. I reach for him once he's no longer pressed to me, searching for the other things I desperately want to feel, like the solid shape of his chest, under his shirt. He's just wearing a thin sort of item of clothing, I think, no coat, just as I'd hoped. And when I wave my hands around in the air I get little fleeting impressions of his body.

He's knelt astride my thighs, torso ramrod straight over me, and I know this because my hand glances against the taut muscles of his abdomen. I flutter my fingers over him, searching and searching, then finally find other things, further up.

Like his incredible chest. Oh Lord have mercy, is it

ever incredible – sort of dense and so much more powerful seeming without the ability to see. When I look at him in the hallway or through windows, I see Ivan – cautious, closed, careful. But when I feel him, he's this overwhelming creature, big and beautiful. It's a primal thing, so raw and almost scary.

But here, I'm allowed to be scared. It's safe to be that way, to be thrilled, and that's a great feeling.

Though it's a better one when he eases my hands away from him. He does it slowly, without insisting upon the move. And once he's done, he trails his own hands down over my body from my throat to my stomach, passing oh-so-sensitive things in between.

I jerk when his palms slide over my breasts, though really it's the way he does it that affects me. He's firm without being too forceful, greedy without going too far. I feel the taut curve between his thumb and forefinger, pressing into the shape of them, mapping them out, before he slides on down.

It's sort of like he's cupping my whole body as he goes. I'm contained by his hands, closed in by them; I'm a series of details that he's uncovering one by one. Like the way my breasts curve outwards slightly at the edges, when I lay down – I think he likes that. I think he likes how my waist feels – almost circled by his two massive hands – before those two hands come apart to cover the swell of my hips.

At which point, I expect him to do more. Start taking

off my clothes, maybe – a thing that seemed horrifying an hour ago but is now a near necessity. I'm dying for him to do it, because, really, what do I have to worry about? I'm secure behind the sanctity of the blindfold. I don't have to see his expression when he sees me, or look at myself while he does it.

I can just feel his hands fondling and stroking me, and imagine he's appreciative.

Until he speaks and spoils the illusion.

'I didn't think you'd be like this,' he says, while a dozen flaws crowd their way into my head. I'm *too* sloppy, *too* slovenly. I didn't do my shoulder exercises or my waist crunches or my breast tighteners, and now I'm all wrong.

'Like what?' I ask, though my head tells me not to. No one wants to hear that they need to buy the new breast-hardening system from ExtremeBody.com.

'So soft,' he says, and there it is. Like pudding, I think, but he proves me wrong again. 'Sometimes I think I see angles underneath your clothes, things to ward people off. The spike of an elbow or the jut of your hip. But you're not like that at all. You're so, so …'

He pauses, then, only this time my brain doesn't fill in a bunch of bad words for him.

I know what's coming now. I can hear it in his voice, as it struggles to get the feeling out. It's what he wants, I think. It's what he longs for.

Just this:

'… inviting.'

As though being that way is as rare as a precious stone from a world we've never been to. It doesn't even really exist for him, out there in the outer reaches of space. He can't even imagine what it looks like, until it's right there in front of him.

And even then he seems to doubt it.

'Is that what you are, Abbie?' he asks, though he doesn't need to. I was five seconds away from reaching for him anyway, now I'm just going to do it. I put my hands out – surer, this time, and without that nervous flutter – and find the waistband of his trousers. The slope of his abdomen.

And this time, he doesn't stop me. I hear him sigh, instead, soft and so good. That body of his leaning ever so slightly into my touch. Though of course with Ivan, leaning ever so slightly is more like going absolutely nuts. I can almost feel the greed vibrating off him, before he even says the words.

'I want you. I want you. I want to let you in, too.'

It's like being offered food for the first time. I'm starving for it, ravenous for it and, when he's done, I push for more. I show him how welcoming I can be, in kisses pressed to his belly, beneath his shirt. In the long slow slide of my tongue around his taut little navel, and the ridged shapes of his every muscle – all of it enhanced by this sightlessness.

I can't see what he looks like. I have to taste him and smell him and feel him, and, oh, all of those things are so good. There's a slight tang of salt that lets me know he's sweating from this close contact, and I can feel his stomach muscles jumping beneath this suddenly so intimate touch.

All of these clues, I think. All of these clues. I'm Poirot in the parlour, waiting for him to confess and prove me right. And the best part is: he does.

'I've never let anyone be like this with me,' he says, while I buzz all over at words like those. He could arouse me with a letter from the gas board, I think. He's arousing me now, even though he's barely doing anything at all.

He's just keeping perfectly still, as I explore him the way he explored me a moment earlier – though, I confess, I go a little further. He didn't go underneath my clothes, but I get underneath his. I find his too tight little nipples and remember how much he seemed to enjoy playing with them.

So I do. I try pinching them between thumb and forefinger, rubbing them a little, just the way I like, back and forth, and then soft, soft on the very tip. Of course I can't use sight as a guide. I can't see if he likes this thing more than that thing, pinching more than stroking, pleasure more than pain. I have to go by the rhythms of his body. The way his chest heaves just a little when I scratch my fingernail over one. Or the sound he makes, ohhhh, the sound he makes when I wet my finger and apply that slickness to those spiky tips …

It's identical to the one I made when he urged me to do the same. Throaty and half stunned, so eager for more – or at least I think it's eager for more, until he claps his hands over mine. He stops me again, forces my hands down, only this time he's far quicker about it.

His movements have lost their easiness, their deliberation. He doesn't urge me down on the bed, he moves away, and then all I can see and hear is the sudden space between us. There's nothing there when I wave my hands in front of me, and no words of comfort from him, and when he finally does return it's in a great rush of activity.

I can't keep up with most of it. He pulls my jumper over my head and unzips my skirt, and before I know it I'm nearly bare in front of him. I can feel the air on my skin in all the places I don't want to be – my too-rounded stomach and my big clumsy breasts and my thighs, oh God, my thighs.

So it's a surprise, really, when he follows all of this with his mouth. I'm still stuck in self-conscious mode, wanting to cover myself but not quite daring to. But he's busy not giving a single fuck, that perfect Cupid's bow mouth of his finding all the places I'm most nervous about.

He goes for my waist, first – that curve he seemed to so appreciate, and now quite obviously does. I can't deny it, even with my eyes covered and no real words spoken between us. He likes how I curve just there. He likes my stomach, and tells me so by rubbing his face against it, just as he did with my hand.

Though it's more intense here. My body clenches all over to feel him doing it, and when my muscles let out they leave behind a thick ebb of pleasure. I'm awash in it, just knowing how soft he actually finds me.

Soft enough to bury his face in me. Soft enough to feel me all over, all at once. His hands slip inside my panties, over the curve of my ass, and then a second later they're roaming my back, while his mouth finds my stiff nipples unerringly, through the flimsy material of my bra.

And once he's got them he goes for more than the little tentative strokes I offered.

He sucks one tight point into his mouth, using the material there to make things so, so much worse. It rubs like velvet over that little bud, getting wetter and wetter as he goes, until finally he can't take it anymore. There's too much in the way, too much teasing, I think.

He wants to feel me properly, and he does. He yanks one cup of my bra down, and then it's skin to skin. That's his tongue I can feel, easing so slickly over my stiff nipple. Circling it quickly, before ending with one long, agonising suck.

Oh God, I swear I didn't know something so slight and simple could feel so good. I've never had someone pay such dedicated attention to a part of my body I didn't much care about, until right now. Why would I? Most men don't, once they've gotten themselves as worked up as he clearly is.

Because he is. Even if he's trying to deflect attention away from himself, I can hear it in his panting breath and feel it in the heat he's giving off, not to mention that hard thing I can make out, ever so slightly pressing against my thigh.

But he doesn't seem all that interested in it. His focus is so overwhelmingly on me I find myself flailing, unsure of even the simplest things – like, what do I do with my hands? Is it OK if I put them on his back? He didn't appear to like me roaming free all over him before, but maybe it's different now that he's making out with my tits.

It certainly *feels* different. His greediness alone is turning everything on its head. He pulls my bra off without asking and kisses my mouth without any kind of deliberation, and when I spread my legs – involuntarily, I swear it's involuntary – he hardly hesitates.

He slides his whole hand over my swollen mound, through the material of my panties.

Of course I moan. And maybe I jerk a little, too – though there's nothing I can do about it. I'm still stuck in a space where the slightest touch is too much, where kissing feels like fucking, and licking my nipples burns a hole right through my body.

I don't know how to process this. The move is just so

open, so *lewd*, and, though he doesn't actually touch any of the good stuff, everything feels him, anyway. My clit jumps at the barest hint of his fingers; my pussy clenches around nothing.

Even the shame of all of that *wetness* – all of the wetness he must be able to feel – doesn't turn me off. I don't care. I'm rubbing myself against that hand before he's even progressed to anything more, all of my thoughts consumed by those few millimetres. Those tiny little millimetres between his fingertips and my slippery slit ... how he could just ease my panties aside and work through my slick folds ...

I almost tell him to do it I'm so far gone.

Just go on, I think, just press a little, rub a little.

But he simply carries on with whatever this is: his mouth on mine, hot and delicious. That big hand cupping me between my legs in a way that's both maddening, and somehow so lovely. I'm safe like this, being held like this. I'm safe in his arms. There's no need to be anxious over all the things he may or may not do, or all the things I don't know how to do.

I bask, for a moment, in bliss.

And then it's right back to crazy, stuttering pleasure and blind panic – in this case, literally. I can't see what he's doing but I can feel it, and I know what it's likely to be. Men don't kiss their way down your body because they're aiming for your feet.

Or so I've heard. From other people. Other people who've actually experienced oral sex, and are not mortally afraid of it. In all fairness to me, I have good reason for this completely irrational fear. I might accidentally kill him if he does this to me.

I can't even take nipple licking, for God's sake. My thighs want to clamp around his head before he's even worked his way down there and, once they do, I fear they'll decapitate him. I fear I'll claw at his back like a rabid animal, or maybe make noises that disturb all of the wonderful quiet of his perfect apartment.

So it's not a surprise that I put a hand over his when he hooks one finger under the elastic of my panties. It's just a surprise that he says something when I do. I didn't say anything to him when he made me stop. I didn't think that was allowed, but apparently it is.

'It's OK, it's OK,' he says. 'I just want to make you feel good. Don't you want me to make you feel good?'

'There's no real answer to that.'

'Sure there is: *yes*.'

'Would you have said yes if I told you I wanted to keep touching you?' I ask, and I'm certain I've got him there. He falls silent for a few seconds, as though he's stumped.

Which only makes it more shocking when I suddenly feel his tongue running over the seam of my sex, through my panties. I even feel the curl he gives to it as he gets to my clit – just enough to send a jolt of pleasure through me.

'Probably not.'

'Why?'

'Because I prefer touching you. There's nothing quite like seeing your back arch when I find your swollen clit. Ohhhh, it's so swollen. I can feel it without really doing anything to you at all. Just a brush of my tongue and it's right there, right through the material of your underwear.'

He's not wrong. I think his breath might put me over the edge every time I feel it ghost hotly over that sensitive place.

'And your voice … I love hearing your voice. It's better than it was over the phone – so breathless, so full of lust.' He says the word 'lust' the way other people might say 'holy high heaven of everything I want'. Like it's something magical, almost unattainable, forbidden. 'And your skin when you flush so prettily … you like it when I do this to you, Abbie?'

'What if I say no?' I ask, though really I'm wondering what he would answer if I asked him the same thing.

'If you say no, I'll stop,' he says, but I can still feel that hot breath ghosting over my pussy. I'm still squirming because of it. 'We can talk about sandwiches again if you like. Or poets. What was that one you mentioned again?'

I'm so far gone I have to wait until he fills the blank in for me.

'"I like my body when it's with your body",' he says, while I writhe in agony. He's teasing me, and he so knows it. He has to know it, right?

'E.E. Cummings,' I manage, but it's not without a price. In order to get words out, I have to let my hips lift towards him, just a little. I have to take my hand away from his so he can just go ahead if he wants.

Who cares about things like resistance when he can tease like this and talk like this and make me so crazy? Who cares about anything then? I just want him to lick my pussy, even if the thought is as terrifying as it is delicious.

'He has a point, Cummings,' he says, the contrast between his patient, almost diffident words and his heated actions like a knife in my gut. That's where the tease lies: between talk about poetry and his fingers easing under the elastic of my panties. He's going to slide them down now, I think, while he gives me his opinion on a line of verse. 'My body is easier to like, when it's with your body.'

I turn blindly towards the sound of his voice, seeking the expression I can't see. Without it, it's impossible to tell how serious he is. How much he believes what he's saying. I mean, no one could hate the shapes his body makes. It's flawless, it's golden and glorious. I have dreams about it, and I don't mind telling him so.

'Are you seriously saying you don't like what you've got? You know that I'm wet, now, thinking about what you've got.'

'I thought you were wet because that kiss was so intense I wanted to fall right into it and never come back up. Or maybe because I took those sweet little nipples in my mouth, and sucked on them. Feels good, right? Having a mouth on you there.'

Him saying all of this probably wouldn't be so tormenting if he wasn't peeling my panties off as he speaks. He eases them down an inch at a time, making sure I can feel the silk sides of them rubbing against my thighs, the insides of my knees, my shins.

And then once they're off, he parts my legs in this casual, easy sort of way. Like it's no big deal really. It's no big deal that I'm blindfolded, and that I can't even make out how terrible I must look. He's just going to stare at my pussy, while he talks up a fucking storm.

'Ohhhh, look at you. Look how wet you are, Abbie. If you could only see what I can see: all of your soft, soft curves, and how flushed you are ... and then your legs so sweetly spread for me. Your slippery sex, so wet and ready for me. I can see it glistening all over your clit and down to your hot little pussy ...'

He finishes his sentence with one trailing finger, passing over the things he's just mentioned. My breasts, my hips, every turn and hill of my body ... and finally my slick folds, parting them as he goes. Not quite putting any real pressure on, but, ohhhh, the sensation is so good all the same. It's better in fact. My hips buck up to get more of it, and when they do …

Oh, when they do …

He uses the angle of my body to just slide inside me, all the way in to the webbing between his fingers. Slow and easy, like everything else he's doing, but so electric because of that patience. I feel every little part of him going in. I feel the rough hump of his knuckle and how slick I am around him, how easily I part for the intrusion, where usually I'm tight and tense and it's always painful.

It's always like something shoving into me, rather than what this is: a slippery glide that ends on me moaning.

'You like that, huh? Want more?' he asks, but he doesn't wait for me to answer. He just interprets the jerk of my hips, which say yes for me. I'm almost fucking myself on him before he even adds a second finger, or tells me how amazing it looks. Like this, like this: 'Oh you take that so good, baby. That's it, that's it – work yourself on me.'

God. God. Does he know how crazy his talk makes me? The dirtier he gets, the thicker his accent is, and the thicker his accent is, the more I moan. The more I rut against him. It's a vicious circle, which ends with me saying something very bad indeed.

'Let me suck your cock while you do that,' I tell him, and I don't even stop there. 'Let me touch you, let me stroke you ... please. Please, I just want to feel your body, God, your body. You have to know how incredible it is. Let me show you.'

His hand gets a little rougher, between my legs, those maddening fingers becoming more like a fuck than anything else. It's good though. It's so good, and not just because of the rough bursts of sensation it produces. There's also the motivation behind it:

To stop me begging for things he kind of wants to give, now, but can't.

He's breaking, it seems. Just a little more might do it ...

'Don't you want to feel my mouth on you, while you make me come? Because, ohhh, you're gonna make me come so hard. Please, Ivan. Please,' I try, but he still doesn't make a move. He just keeps up that relentless pressure, and soon I know it will be too late. I'm close to the edge, and, once I've gone over, I'll be too embarrassed to ask him for things like this.

And I think he knows it.

'Let me,' I say, only this time he answers with a little lick.

Right between my legs. Right over my swollen, sensitive clit, and then, just when I want to cry foul and call him a cheat, he does it again. He pins my hips when I

105

try to jerk away, and holds me fast when I protest, and after that he's free to work on me in any way he wants. He can rub that killer tongue over my little bud, and pump into my clenching pussy as he does it.

And I can't make a single demand once he's there. All I can manage is a kind of rough blurt of air and a lot of gasping, followed by my hands that seem to want to clench in his hair. I get hold of it tightly and squeeze, but it doesn't really help.

I'm going to come, and after a second I tell him so. It's the only words I can get out, as rude and wrong as they are.

'Ohhhh, yeah, right there, right there, lick my pussy,' I tell him, as though I never thought there'd be a problem with him doing this at all. I wasn't nervous before. I just didn't know how fucking amazing this would feel – oh, amazing enough to make me lose my mind and spill out things like this: 'God, I'm going to do it, I'm going to do it.'

I don't even know what *doing it* means.

And, apparently, neither does he.

'Doing what?' he asks, in between kisses.

Only it's the sort of kisses you couldn't tell your mother about over dinner. Kisses for my clit, for my pussy. Kisses that leave me hovering on the brink.

'Orgasm,' I say. 'I'm having an orgasm.'

And then the pleasure washes over me in a bright,

tight wave. It starts at my clit and bursts outwards, but there's an underlying note to it, an intensity to it that I don't quite know how to process. He's been rubbing at something inside me, something I've never really been able to uncover myself, and when the pleasure lets go there's a dull pulse underneath it. It's like a weight, dragging that wave of sensation back. It pulls it in until I can hardly bear it, until I want to tell him no, no, that's too much.

Though I doubt he'd listen. I can hear him groaning, too, over my own embarrassingly guttural grunts, like maybe he enjoys watching me lose it this way. In fact, I know he enjoys watching me lose it, because once I come around from this incredible orgasm, once I realise I've curled myself into a ball halfway up the bed, and that my ears are kind of ringing and my body is in spasm, I can hear him.

He's masturbating.

He's masturbating and, even more delightful, he's saying things in Russian. Dirty-sounding things that drag another little spike of pleasure out of an orgasm that should be long done.

'Tell me what you're saying,' I ask him. 'Tell me.'

But of course he can't. He's now in the position I was in five seconds ago: struck almost mute by sensation. Even the Russian words fall away, and then I'm trapped in a sightless world made up of his breathing, harsh and frantic. The sound of his hand on his cock, slick-clicking back and forth, back and forth.

Lord, how I wish I could see him. I wish I could just rip this blindfold off, but I know the effect it would have. He'd back off, I know it, though I'm still not quite sure why. Because the closeness of this and the closeness of me seeing him would just be too much together? Because he mysteriously hates his own body?

Even though it doesn't sound like he hates it now. The stroke of his hand speeds up, and so do his near shame-less moans. It's like he can't help it and, of course, if he can't help this … if he can't stop this … maybe he won't be able to stop a few other things too.

Like my hand tentatively reaching out for him. Just for his arm, maybe, or possibly his chest. Perhaps if I start out someplace innocuous, he'll let me progress.

Or at least that's the theory, until I actually make contact. I think I find his elbow, but he goes stiff anyway. He flinches as though I've struck him, and that maddening, delicious sound I can hear stops.

Then just as suddenly resumes. Oh, it *resumes*. Is there any sweeter sound than that? I can hear his breathing getting more unsteady and there's a protest hanging on his tongue, I know there is. But he doesn't really try to stop me.

He lets me run my hand up his arm, over that thick bicep, the touch made easier by the perspiration that's lightly coating him. Then I move on, upwards first. Upwards is nice and safe, and he doesn't have to worry about it. Who cares if I touch his shoulder?

Apart from me?

Because, God, it drives me nuts to feel him like this. His shoulder is like something carved out of wood, solid and unyielding. And his throat ... ohhhh, his throat. Would it be so wrong if I just leaned forwards and bit him there, where the flesh feels firmest? He'd probably send me away and never let me come back, but at this point I'm not sure I care.

I want to taste him. I need to taste him.

Don't stop me, I think at him, and by some miracle, he doesn't. He must be able to see my every move – I'm not being crafty in the slightest – but he lets me slowly lean in. He lets me put my mouth on his chest, and then, after a bit of manoeuvring, his throat.

I don't bite as I'd been intending to.

I lick, and feel him shudder for my trouble.

'Abbie,' he says, but there's no real resistance in his voice. The word is almost a sigh, and he doesn't stop the stroke over his cock. I know he doesn't. I'm so close now that I can actually feel the brush of the back of his hand over my thigh as he slides it up and down. And when I shift a little ... that's the head of his cock just touching my bare belly.

It's obvious it is, because after a second I can make

out the slipperiness of his pre-come. He's marking my skin, making it shiny. And he's moaning and shuddering and leaning into my teasing mouth as he does it.

It's almost like a victory. I just triumphed over the opposing team – the one called *his bizarre hang-ups* – and now I get to run my hands *down* his body. I've won the game; I've got to try for more. I've got to rub my palms over his rigid abdomen, and map out his hips the way he did mine.

They don't jut the way mine do, but there's that lovely slant of muscle sliding down from them, like an arrow pointing at his groin. I remember it from the window, but it's even better beneath my touch – so firm, and so slick with perspiration.

Followed by the things beneath it.

I hardly dare touch him there, but his lack of resistance makes me bold, as bold as he was with me. He didn't wait when I held back, so why should I wait here? Why should I be nervous? Why is my heart beating so hard and fast?

Because it is. I'm surprised *he* can't hear it, thundering away in my chest, and all for something so simple again. Just my hand over his hand, as he strokes himself. And then, when he lets me, a little more. I press my thumb against the rigid base of his cock so that I'll have the memory of his actual flesh when I come away from this.

After all, this may be the limits of what I get. He's

stopped making any noises – as though he's holding his breath, maybe – and any second he's going to tell me that I should stop. I've gone too far, pushed him too hard, and I've got to consider that.

How would I feel if he did the same?

I'd be devastated; I'd be terrified. I've got to say sorry. In fact, I come so close to doing just that I almost taste the words in my mouth. I'm inches away from moving my hand and shifting back down the bed when he takes his own hand away.

And puts it over mine.

'Like this,' he says, and this time the sense of victory is so keen I could cry over it. He's not resisting me; he's urging me on. He even kisses me as he works my hand over his solid cock, like everything is fine and we're both so normal. We're completely normal, and I can touch him and put my arms around him and stroke him in intimate places.

No barriers get in the way now. I'm so close to him I can feel the way his body is shaking all the way through mine. And after a while those sounds he was making a moment ago go through me too. He moans right into my mouth, as he forces my hand in a steady, driving rhythm, almost too tight for me to bear it, but so arousing even so.

I can feel him swelling under my grip and I know he's going to come. He's going to come for me, with me touching him, and my mouth on his. All those times through the window, so far away, narrowed down to this:

His face pressed tight into my shoulder, as he finally lets go.

Chapter Eight

It takes me about an hour of lazing around in a pleasure-stuffed stupor to realise something pretty sad: I got more pleasure out of a blindfolded handjob with him than I did out of every previous relationship I've ever had. We haven't even had sex, and yet somehow I'm utterly satisfied. I'm a cat, fat with food and sunning myself in the heat of whatever this is. This ... thing. This ... relationship.

Though I can't really call it that, can I?

People are usually allowed to look at each other full in the face when they're in a relationship, but somehow I still don't feel comfortable taking the blindfold off. Baby steps, I think. If he moves too fast I might run away, and if I move too fast he might run away, so I guess we just have to take our time.

Crawl towards each other in stages, until finally …

'I love you, Abbie.'

All right. That wasn't what I was expecting. And I show this total lack of expectation by vacating the little comfy space I've made in the crook of his arm, to stare at him sightlessly through my blindfold.

It feels somewhat less erotic when we're just having a conversation.

In fact, it feels kind of ridiculous, and this ridiculousness shows itself in the little laugh he lets out. He even reaches forwards and pulls the thing off, as though me seeing him doesn't really matter at all anymore.

And then I go and spoil it with my giant blundering awfulness.

'Did you really just say that?'

Why do I have to be incredulous? We've practically been weird boyfriend and girlfriend for over a month. We've had more intense conversations about feelings and issues than I've ever had with anyone, not to mention all the talk about BLTs.

His stance on tomatoes alone means we should be married by now. Always cherry tomatoes, never beef. Slice them as thin as the big ones, and then go to town on that bad boy.

Apart from the obvious psychological problems, he's the perfect man.

'I have a feeling it's weird that I did.'

'It's kind of weird that you can say those words, but you can't have me looking at you during sex. Or touching you during sex for that matter.'

'Why?'

He sounds genuinely puzzled, and almost bizarrely unconcerned. He's not even really concentrating on the conversation – he's running the backs of his fingers over the long section of hair that's fallen over my shoulder, watching it lift and then drop, lift and then drop.

'Because loving someone is a lot more intimate than giving someone a handjob.'

'And you think I have problems with intimacy?'

'Don't you?' I ask, but when he flicks his gaze up to mine my question is answered. I can almost feel how much I mean to him, every time he looks into my eyes. It burns out through them – it has ever since the hallway.

And he's never shied away from showing it.

'I struggle with physical things. Not emotions.'

I have to ask. Don't I? I'd be a fool if I didn't.

'Why?' I ask, while my head fills with every terrible thing it could be. What makes someone afraid to be touched, but fearless when it comes to something I can't even say yet? I feel it, but I can't say it.

He could still turn out so wrong, after all. Maybe he doesn't really want me in the messy state I'm in. Maybe he wants to mould me until I fit seamlessly into his touch-less world, both of us dancing around each other for the rest of our lives, with punishments for every transgression I make.

I get a punch, for accidentally grabbing his ass. A kick in the stomach for an elbow brush in bed.

Christ.

'I don't know,' he says, but he's lying. And though his next words are caring and sharing and they go some way to make up for that, the lie sticks in the back of my mind. 'But this is the only time I've ever done anything like this. I've never done any of those things with someone I didn't pay first, and, when I have done it in the past, I paid them to force me into it.'

'Is that what it takes then? Force?'

'Not when it's you, no. You persuade me. You erase everything that holds me back, and replace it with something else.'

'I do? Seems like a tall order for someone as nothing as me.'

'You think you're nothing, Abbie?' He's not playing with my hair anymore. He's stroking the side of my face, in that same slow, wondering sort of way. 'You, who didn't look away? You're still looking now, though I've done my best to stop you. Nothing I've said has put you off, even though there's a hole in your body where your trust used to be. Who wouldn't love you, Abbie, knowing that?'

I don't know if he expects me to answer. He should know that I can't.

'Don't cry, my lovely girl. Don't cry,' he says, and then he kisses my face. He kisses me close up, with my eyes on him and his eyes on me, and suddenly I don't need to cry anymore.

I'm halfway to OK.

* * *

He doesn't stop there. Somehow I think I expected him to – that, when I returned from this dreamland of sex and satisfaction and long low talks about feelings, everything would just flip back to the way it was. Cold nights, the store, occasional glimpses of him through my window.

But he exceeds my wildest hopes in every way. He sends me a note the next day: splinters of poems, the sorts of things I thought only existed in fairytales. He makes a game of it, where I have to guess the source of such lovely words: *I can only be complete when I am with you*, he sends me, and I uncover it quickly, avidly.

My reward is another inch of his body, another island on the map of him. He lets me kiss his chest for guessing Shakespeare, and lick the length of his cock for Rossetti. No more blindfolds, but he's skittish, and he hides said skittishness beneath a kind of hunger for me that I can't easily fight.

I'm not prepared for it. I'm used to tepid, or cruel, indifference.

117

He gives me long, slow kisses all over my body, from the innocuous curve at the nape of my neck, all the way down to things I didn't even know existed. There's a place just between my thigh and my pussy, and when he licks me there I can't control myself. I fist my hands in his short hair, I beg him to stop, I beg him to carry on.

And the same goes double when he buries his face somewhere very rude indeed.

He cares if I touch his shoulder in a slightly filthy way. But apparently he doesn't care about something as lewd as licking me between the cheeks of my arse. He just does it, like it means nothing. I shouldn't be startled, or try to escape up the bed.

I should just enjoy him *rimming me*.

'OK,' I think I say. 'OK.'

But it's not OK. I'm trapped between a fizzing, giddy sort of pleasure and absolute shame – though I'm not sure which is turning me on more. The heat from my face seems to have slid down my body, and is now between my legs. All I can feel is the slipperiness of his tongue wriggling and squirming against my tightly clenched hole, igniting nerve endings I didn't know existed. Most of them spark and send direct messages to my clit. Some of them make me go rigid all over and try to resist.

But I can't, I can't.

'Ohhhh God, yeah,' I say, because really what else can I do? If I say no he might stop. He stopped the other day when I begged him not to push me into a second orgasm, right after the first.

And then he made me tell him a safe word, just in case no doesn't really mean yes.

He gives me a lot of things like that, when I really think about it. Caring things, loving things … crazy sex acts that make me insane.

'That good?' he asks me, in between those long wet licks. I'm so slippery back there, he could probably ease a finger into that tight passage, if he really wanted to, but I'm not going to suggest it.

I'll just let him know he's on the right path, and see where it goes.

'Yeah.'

'You want me to do more?'

He's a fucking genius, seriously. And a mind reader. And, ohhh, I love him I love him I love him, just *say it*. I almost did it on the phone the other night when he signed off that way, so casual and without expectation. *I love you, my one.*

But instead I just went with a lame, weak: *You're my one, too.*

'Yes.'

'Like this?' he asks, and I hold my breath, waiting for it.

It's almost a disappointment when he just eases a finger into my pussy, as slow and careful as he was the first time.

Though with the added bonus of his mouth against my arse, as he does it. Oh, that makes the sensation a little different, all right. I jerk a little to feel it, and moan his name. Then again when he finds my clit, too, with the eight hundred fingers he shouldn't actually have. Seriously, how does he manage to target every part of me all at once?

I can feel him doing this in my *teeth*. I have to grab a hold of his headboard, and hold on tight. No one could take this much sensation all at once. No one.

And yet when it crests, I'm there for it. I let it roll through my body and right out of my mouth: *Ahhhh, yes, yes, I'm coming, I'm coming*, I tell him, and he tells me things in response. *Oh you're so sensitive, baby*, he tells me. *You're so easy to push over the edge. Yeah, yeah, that's right. Come all over my hand. Come all over my face.*

It's not hard to oblige him.

It's never hard to oblige him. I don't feel nervous anymore, getting out of my clothes. I tear them all off before I'm even through his door. I don't mind if he wants to kiss me between my legs; I'm not ashamed of how hard and fast he makes me come.

But I *am* ashamed that I can't do the same for him.

He won't even let me cuddle him after he's done, because by this point he knows where that's going to go. I'll try to leverage the hugging into a crafty slide down his body, for the blowjob he seems almost mortally afraid of getting.

'You know I could pin you down if you wanted me to. Like he did?' I say, to his retreating back. He disappears into the bathroom and, I've got to admit, it's not really a comfort that he doesn't shower immediately, like this is filthy.

Mainly because I wish that thought didn't keep occurring to me.

'Is that what you think I need?'

'Well, since most of you is a guessing game it's kind of hard to say what it is you need. And you did send me that tape. Maybe you were trying to give me a clue.'

'Or maybe I just wanted to give you something that would make you feel less vulnerable. Less like I needed to be a big man with you.'

I think I'd kind of known that. But still, it's lovely to hear him spell it out.

'If that was your intention, that's quite a gesture. I kind of think it's more than that though.'

'Yeah? What else do you think it is?'

'I think you wanted to give me a part of yourself. A part you seem to find so hard to talk about you're having this conversation with me from another room.'

121

'I needed to piss.'

'You're not pissing.'

'My teeth needed cleaning. My hair needed brushing. There's a rug in here that's not straight.'

'See, you think you're being funny. But all I'm wondering now is why the neatness, too? Why does everything have to be in its place, perfectly ordered? My ex-boyfriend liked things perfectly ordered, too, and it didn't turn out so well for me.'

The silence that then stretches out has a pulse. It's heavy and alive and I don't like it at all. I wish I hadn't said that, but it's there and it's out now.

'Is that how you really feel? That I'd hurt you like that?'

He comes and stands in the doorway and leans against the frame, which takes a bit of the sting out of this idea I've dragged us both into. And I try to alleviate it further by saying what I really feel: 'No.'

But, oh, it's still a fist around my heart, when he says: 'I like things like this because once something happened to me that I couldn't stop. I couldn't control it. But I don't *want* to be this way, Abbie. I want everything that this is not, that I am not. I don't want that one thing to govern my life anymore, and that's what you are. You're anything but that. And I just want you to take my hand and help me out of this maze. I need out of this –'

I cut him off. I have to. This fist around my heart is killing me dead.

'I got you,' I tell him. 'Any time you want me to help you out of this, I'm there. Because, God knows, you've helped me. I didn't know people could be the way you are ... you're so careful with me. I don't know why I said that about my ex-boyfriend, I don't.'

'Because you're scared.'

'I'm always scared.'

'That makes two of us then,' he says, as he crosses to the bed. I've drawn up my knees to my chest, but he eases them back down again.

And then he takes my hands in his and puts them over his heart.

'Anything you want, I'll give you,' he says. 'That's how I climb out of this. I think about you, and all of the things you could ask me to do. Just ask me, Abbie.'

'Can I kiss you?'

'Yes,' he tells me, so I do. I touch my lips to his, as chaste as a new maid on her wedding night. And when I ask him if I can hold his face in my hands, he lets me do that too. He lets me run them down from there over his back, stopping just short of something ruder.

'Can I touch you like this?' I ask, and there's some resistance then. Some, but not much. And less of it once I've squeezed that fantastic ass between my greedy fingers.

'Yes,' he tells me, but the word is long and drawn out and he ends his sentence with this: 'Yes, yes, just like that.'

'And what about this?'

I kiss his throat, then thrill to hear more than just an affirmative.

'Bite me,' he says. 'I love being bitten.'

'You do?' I ask, but only because I'm so surprised. I'm surprised he would offer the information; I'm surprised he likes something *so* physical. You can't get much more into someone than half an inch deep with your teeth.

But he just nods, eyes reduced to smoky slits. And there's more, too.

'I like to bite, too, but I didn't want to scare you away with something like that,' he says, and this is the point, I know. This is the part where I can show him how full he's made that hole through me, where trust once was.

'You can,' I tell him. 'I don't mind.'

And I do it as casually as he had seemed, stood in that doorway. Though he looks very far from it now. His body has gone all tense, and his face has gone all tense, and he doesn't seem certain when he answers.

'Are you sure?'

'Yes.'

'And you'll say the word if you don't like it?'

'I'll say the word if you don't do it soon,' I say, and that's the thing that gets him going. Just a little humour laid over the top of everything, to make it lighter. To make it sweeter. He's not going to hurt me, I think, he's not going to at all.

And he doesn't. He makes it feel sooooo *good*.

It's more than good in fact. His teeth just graze my skin, close to some sensitive spot where my shoulder and neck meet, and I gasp over the sensation. The hint of pain, the burst of pleasure ... and most of all, oh most of all, the sense of the care he's taking ...

I love him for all of those things.

I love him.

'I love you,' I say, but he doesn't make me feel raw or wrong about it. He just presses me tighter, tighter, until there really is no space between us. He's biting and kissing at my neck, and I'm biting and kissing at his. I can feel his erection rubbing against my belly and in a little while, I know ...

We're going to have sex.

That's what we're building towards right now. That's how things happen when you're normal: you let someone else touch you, and that same someone else touches you. And then finally, finally, you both lie down together, bodies entwined.

He hasn't even got his eyes closed anymore. We're looking at each other as he eases me open with those clever fingers. And we continue to do so as I cup his stiff cock, rubbing and rubbing at him until he's beyond ready. He's all the way over into ravenous, though it's not because of the sensation I know.

It's because I hold his face in my hands and tell him he's my one.

'You're mine,' he says. 'You're mine.'

And I am. I spread my legs around his body, barely able to wait for him to put the condom on. I don't even know where he's gotten one from, in all honesty, but the thought only urges my arousal on. He must have known things were coming to this, I think. He hasn't shied away from it. He's letting me run my hands all over his body and his body is right over mine, and then I feel it.

I feel the head of his cock, stroking through my slick folds.

'Are you sure?' he says, but not because he really thinks I'm not. I know why he says it: because I feel suddenly very small, and he feels suddenly very big. His cock nudges against my entrance and then he hesitates, he hesitates.

But I don't.

I don't even think about past pain or that kind of gritted-teeth discomfort. I just arch up against him, and feel that long, solid weight slide inside me. All in one good glide, until I'm full of him, I'm overwhelmed with him. Lord, I didn't think such a thing could feel so freeing. I want to be overwhelmed, I think.

I want him to whisper in my ear the way he then does:

'You're the only woman I've ever done this with.'

And once he's said it I hold him tighter. I rock against him when he can't quite do it; I kiss him when he seems unsure. That hole through me is full up now, and I'm able to do all the things I couldn't, for him. For all the things he can't.

Though, after a while, *can't* becomes *can*. He goes slow at first – testing out the sensation, I think. And when the sensation proves as glorious as I think it does – if his lust-slackened expression is anything to go by – he thrusts a little harder. He jerks his hips a little faster. The rolling fuck he started out with falls away, and I'm left with this:

A sudden franticness that takes my breath away.

'God,' he says. 'God.'

And I agree. Prayers need to be said, for pleasure this thick and fast. I can feel his belly grinding against my clit, and every time he fucks into me – harder than he intends, I know – I have to just hold on. It's like he's forcing sensation through me with each jolting thrust.

I never thought I'd enjoy something like this. But I do. I think I could enjoy anything with him – soft and sweet, rough and hard. I could take him taking me over that table; I could love him telling me what to do. I even love it now, in the middle of this bliss.

'That's it, baby,' he says to me. 'Give it up.'

And I do. I groan his name as my cunt clenches around his cock, my orgasm slow and stuttering at first but then tighter, brighter. I have to dig my nails into his back for the finale – a kind of lowdown kick of pleasure to my gut that has me gasping.

But he doesn't seem to mind. He doesn't mind the gasp and, more importantly, he doesn't mind the nails. *Do it harder*, he groans, which is even better than his last command, really. I get to do something for him instead of taking something for myself. I get to feel his flesh near breaking beneath my touch and, when it does, he arches his back.

He isn't fucking me now. He's rutting into me, eyes narrowed to slits, perspiration glowing all over him. His breath comes in pants, and it turns to something even sweeter when I bite him a little, on top of the nails.

Now he's groaning almost constantly – all of these low ahhhs and uhhs that make me wild. And in between … words for me. Hot words that drive me on and on, until I realise what he's doing.

He's using the pain to get to a place he can't quite reach. He can't quite come, clearly, but every time I give him a little more he gets a little closer. He groans a little harder, he fucks me with a little more abandon, until finally he's half mad with it. His eyes are tight shut and his fists are clenched in the sheets next to my head, but he can't give in.

Emotions are easy, I think. Physical things are hard.

And then I let my nails break through his skin. I let him have something else to concentrate on instead of this panting, desperate pleasure. Instead of his cock inside me and his body pressed to mine and, ohhhh God, yes, then. Then he gives it up for me. I feel it happen the second he does – a kind of shudder goes through him, and then a stillness I can hardly stand.

'Please,' I tell him. 'Please.'

But him obeying isn't enough. He breaks like a dam bursting, mouth open around sounds he can't make, eyes rolling up in his head. That glorious cock swells inside me, as his hips pump and his body shakes through the pleasure.

But still, it can't ever be enough.

Because I know his body and what it needs. He's let me feel him and understand what it takes to make him let go. To have him break over me and inside me, then rest, laughing, against my shoulder.

But I still don't know *why*.

I don't know why he needs to be bloody, before he gives me everything he's got.

Chapter Nine

I know I shouldn't need to know. But I do all the same. I think about it after we've had sex; I think about it during. He falls asleep right up against my body, uncaring about the lack of space between, but I still think about it.

And he still won't tell me.

Or more: I broach the subject, and he changes it so deftly I forget what I was even saying. In my defence, it's hard to remember with his face between my thighs. It's hard to remember when he lets me blindfold him, before running my hand all over his body. He balks at the strangest things: a kiss on the insides of his elbows, a lick over the muscular length of his inner thigh, but not for a finger between the cheeks of his arse.

Abrupt rudeness makes him crazy and acquiescent, tentative deliberation gives him time to think, to consider ...

But what exactly is he considering? I don't know, I don't know. And the more time I spend with him, the more the idea drives me mad. I'm Bluebeard's wife, unable to sleep for the thought of what's behind his locked doors, and, to make matters worse, he actually has one. He doesn't use the walk-in closet. He uses a wardrobe.

But the closet is still here. And the door to it is always locked.

As though he needs to keep the dead body of his wife in, in case she decides to haul her rotten carcass out of there and across the carpet to me.

Seriously. Is it any wonder I can't sleep? Is it any wonder I spend my time in his apartment, staring at that door through the darkness? Nobody wants to be murdered by someone's dead wife. And if this is all just my craziness, if this is all just that hole through my middle trying to force my trust back out again, well, isn't that better?

I'll open the door and find nothing there, and then the hole will be filled and sealed for good. I won't have to worry. We'll keep crawling towards some kind of shaky happiness. I mean, yesterday we actually took a bath together, in the same room, while looking at each other. We've got to be almost there.

Or does the fact that I'm trying to prise open his door with a credit card say otherwise? He left me in the apartment this morning – alone. He's gone out to run errands, to talk with some software developer, to cover the body of his dead wife with lime. Fuck, I don't know.

So I'm doing this. I'm doing it.

And then it opens, and I don't want to do it anymore. Thinking about using a crowbar to prise someone's secrets out of them is fun in the abstract. But it's not fun when you're actually doing it. There isn't even a dead body in the closet to make me feel better about being a snoop – though there are a lot of other things, instead.

There are a lot of video tapes.

And after a second of feeling bad, I start getting that tight feeling in my chest. The one I used to get when I knew Sid was five minutes from home. The one that happens because that hole in me contracts, and, though I've got kisses and I-love-yous to fill it in, it's still just waiting. It's waiting for this cupboard, filled with home movies featuring God knows what.

For a start: why are they video tapes? He's obviously technologically competent. Shouldn't he be lining his walls with DVDs or flash drives or some other fancy thing that you can store films on? Instead, he's just got this cupboard built out of black plastic, like those vaguely creepy backrooms you used to glimpse in video stores. Everything neatly stacked and arranged, to the point where I can run my hand over the stacks and stacks of tapes and feel only a smooth black slickness.

He's so perfectly ordered, my Ivan. And so perfectly weird. I can't even bear to look at the labels on these videos, for a second, in case they tell me just how weird he is. How weird would be too much? Black and white movies of eyeballs being sliced in two? Crackling images of odd children standing at the ends of corridors?

There are a lot of things that could potentially disturb me forever. And a lot of things that could make me feel awful, forever doing this in the first place. He's got a little TV and VCR set up in the centre of the closet on one of those stands you usually see in schools, and when I pick a tape at random and put it in, it's not anything like what I had thought.

It's a home movie. It's not his psychotic art school project or his sideline in murdering people on camera. It's just a home movie of a little boy in a stripy shirt, running around a garden. Nothing creepy about it, nothing awful. Just this little boy and his funny antics and, oh God, oh God ... then I realise.

It's Ivan.

The little boy Ivan.

All the tapes are of him and his family, being ordinary and cute – apart from his dad's weirdly obsessive approach to capturing memories. I mean, there are a *lot* of tapes in here. Hundreds of them. And they're all labelled the same way: with dates that follow almost every aspect of Ivan's life when he was just a kid.

And, oh, he's so cute. He's so carefree and so open. My heart clenches to see him running across the grass, trailing a kite so colourful it lights up this faded and almost worn-down image. The sun is setting somewhere to his left, and the dying rays pick up little flickers of blond in his curly hair. No sound, but I can hear what he's saying anyway:

Watch this. Watch me.

And then the kite takes off into the darkening sky.

How did everything go so wrong? I was so sure this would be a sign, a foundation for the way he is. Like the signs I give away for free. My jumpers, my hair, my being in here right now searching around for a reason to trust ... all scream about what happened to me. But what happened to Ivan?

These memories are warm and lovely. The only possible clues they give out are to do with watching and being watched, but I can't see how they would have had a negative effect. It's not like his dad is evil and into filming his son in his underwear. In all the tapes, Ivan is fully clothed and completely happy.

And then I see the tape that doesn't have a date on it. The one he's centred on a slightly shorter pile, right in the middle of the room, behind the TV. There are words on this one, words that send a little wave of discomfort through me, despite their innocuousness.

Mum and Dad, it says, and I go all weird inside. I don't want to look, but of course it's too late for that now. Who wouldn't look under these circumstances? Stronger people than me, possibly. People who aren't scared of everything and able to hurt so readily inside for someone they're only just in a relationship with.

Other people probably wouldn't care about that little boy and his kite, but I do. I do, and that's why I put the tape in. I'm not afraid it will be Ivan doing something terrible. I know he isn't now. In fact, I kind of know what I'm going to see before I see it, which mitigates the gut-wrenching shock of it somewhat.

But not by much.

At first it's kind of hard to tell what's happening. Whoever filmed it is doing so through the slats in what looks like a wardrobe or a cupboard of some type, and they're not holding the camera steady. It wobbles up and down throughout, and I have to say I'm kind of glad about that.

I don't really need to see too much of his parents being murdered. It's bad enough knowing that he saw it, that he caught it on camera, while trapped inside somewhere. Did he hide when he heard them coming? I don't know, I don't know, and I can't bear to rewind and see. I can't bear to watch this. One of the blurry, hooded men on-screen struggles with what must be his mother, and I turn it off all in a big rush.

And then I just stand there in this little closet of horrors, trembling all over, with my heart beating in my ears. Did he actually somehow film his parents being murdered? Maybe they were doing something nice before, some lovely family memory. And then a bunch of thieves and thugs broke in and suddenly it's *A Clockwork Orange*. Suddenly it's someone ruined forever in a way I can hardly stand, oh, I can hardly stand it.

Everything he let me do to him, every touch he let me have, every kiss, I thought it was so hard won. But now I see: it's a goddamn miracle that he ever lets me near him at all. It's a miracle that he ever lets anyone near him. I'm surprised he's not paralytic in an asylum some-where, because his blackbird isn't someone being an asshole to him a few times.

It's *his parents being murdered in front of him*.

I don't know what to do.

And I know even less when I turn and he's just stood there in the doorway. I think I actually let out a little frightened sound, as though I really did find his dead wife in here. But once that stupidity is over with, my main instinct is to do something even dafter. I just want to cover him with my body. I want to put my arms around him and never let him go, but of course I can't, I can't.

He looks kind of like he wants to kill me. He'll prob-ably do it out of utter terror, but that's not really the point, is it? I'm still going to die, and, worse, I think I deserve it. I shouldn't have used the crowbar. I shouldn't have let my lack of trust guide me. I should have been a normal person who gradually warmed him until he opened up.

But I'm not a normal person. And so here we are.

'How did you get in here?' he asks, and it's no comfort to me that he sounds almost as marvelling as he does upset. Marvelling just means I've used my prying tools inventively, and not just the actual, literal ones, like the credit card that's still in my hand. I mean the metaphorical ones too.

The ones he's really gutted about.

'I just …' I start, but what can I say? *I just wanted to know you* sounds so lame. *I was scared* sounds even lamer. I don't deserve a proper relationship; I don't deserve this. Which is probably why I don't protest when he tells me he thinks I should go.

I've been deemed unworthy, and now I'm being cast out of the labyrinth of him. And that's OK, that's really OK, because he's probably right. This isn't the bit where I hug him and make everything OK. This is the bit where I accept that I'll never be right or capable of having a relationship, and walk out of the door.

Though once I've done it, I know:

I don't think I can let him go.

Chapter Ten

I dream that he's falling through my fingers. Of course I try to hold on, but it's almost impossible when he's made of nothing. His arms and legs crumple beneath my grip, and before I can do anything the wind catches his papery body, and blows him away.

And I wake up sweating and crying, still completely unsure of what to do. I tried a letter: he didn't reply. I went to my window: he isn't at his. His phone rings and rings until I feel like a maniac again, madly stalking a man who doesn't want to be found.

His door is shut again. He's closed back up. And all because I just had to know, I had to know, oh God, why did I have to know? It doesn't make me feel any better now that I do. Instead, I have more dreams in which he doesn't turn to paper and blow away. He gets murdered in front of me, while I film everything with a video camera.

That one's a real doozy, I tell you. Lord knows what kind of dreams he has on a daily basis, after actually going through something like that. I'm surprised he's functioning at all, but then again he isn't, is he?

He has that cupboard full of video tapes and his clothes all in a row, and prior to me he hired thugs to fake-brutalise him, whenever he wanted a bit of intimacy. He had to be forced into doing anything beyond watching.

And now he won't even watch.

Which is a shame, because I'm more than ready to stand at the window for him now. I'd do anything for him now. I *dream* about doing anything. In some of them, he lets me roam all over his naked body, from that slice of muscle to the jut of his heavy collarbone. And I devour him with my mouth, I do. I taste the glorious curve of his cock, long and smooth and just a little slick at the tip.

Just a little salt-sweet.

In my dreams, he always bucks into my mouth. He resists at first, but then he can't anymore, and those hips lift, forcing him deeper into me. Forcing him over my tongue, filling my mouth – oh God, those dreams are worse than the dying ones. They're like waking up with the belief that someone long dead is still alive.

He's still alive, and he's going to kiss me at any moment. I'll answer the door and there he'll be, just like that longing-filled fantasy I had of our bodies plastered together. Only this time when I imagine it, we're somehow naked the minute he walks through the door. His chest rubs roughly against the tips of my breasts, and similarly I can feel him between my thighs.

I feel his hot, strong cock, like an iron bar against my always overheated pussy, and then he lifts me and simply slides all the way inside. As smooth as he did when we first made love, only sweeter this time because it's a reunion.

It's that bit in the movie when the couple realise all obstacles can be overcome, and then he returns to her and sweeps her into his arms. Which sounds like utter nonsense, now that I'm thinking about it. It sounds like three-day-old garbage, and I suddenly hate Hollywood for doing that to me. The one constant in my life – my love of film – has turned against me in my hour of need.

Or at least I think so. I think so, until I hear my doorbell ring.

There's no one else it could be. No one else in the world. Nobody ever comes to my door; nobody cares where I live. It can't be the mailman or the milkman or someone calling door to door with leaflets.

It has to be Ivan. He read my last note –*Oh my love how you call to me, call to me* – and it made him forgive me. It made him come back to me, to offer a second chance I probably don't deserve. In fact, I definitely know I don't deserve it.

Because it isn't Ivan at the door.

Of course, I try to close it again immediately. But I think it's a mistake that I do. Maybe if I'd paused, and tried to be rational, we could have had a calm conversation first. *Try to see things from my point of view*, I could have said to him. *I ran away from you because you hit me with a hammer.*

But, instead of taking this route, I panic and try to shut him out. I try to act like he's not really there, but naturally he muscles his way in even so. He gets his foot in the door – of course he does – and he laughs in that awful manner of his. Like he's saying: *Oh, Abbie, why do you have to be so silly?*

The answer's obvious. I'm silly because he forces the door open, and once he's inside he grabs me by the hair. He doesn't even pretend he's going to do anything different. He just pulls and pulls until it hurts so bad I have to be on my knees. I have to be.

But I'm not as acquiescent as I used to be about going. I used to cry for him, prettily, but now I know what it's like to cry because someone's been so kind you can't stand it. I know what it's like to cry with joy and relief, and I don't want to cry like this anymore.

I want to punch him in the groin.

So I do.

He isn't expecting it. Of course he isn't. He's halfway through his *do you know how hard it is to forgive you* speech, which doesn't include an encore of intense pain between his legs. His thin-lipped mouth makes this big surprised O, and those dark brows I once thought beautiful draw together.

And that's the last thing I see before I make a run for it.

I barrel down the hallway, not thinking of a coat or my things or where I'm going to run to. I didn't think about it last time either. I just ran and ran and ran and this is where I ended up: almost normal, almost living, almost in a relationship with a man called Ivan.

It's almost like a fairytale, if you blindfold yourself before looking at it.

Except, of course, in this version, the monster is still chasing me through the labyrinth. And there's no escape, no key to press, no lock to find. I bang on doors as I fly down these green tunnels, but no one hears me.

I doubt they would if I used a battering ram and a foghorn. That's the way things are around here, after all: no one hears and, more importantly, no one *sees*. Once I'm outside, all the closed-curtained windows stare down at me, silently mocking me forever thinking I could have a normal life. That I could just escape so easily.

And worst of all, of course, is Ivan's window. As dark

and silent as a tomb, completely impassive as I run around the pool and head for the exit to this little cul-de-sac.

I get close, I'll say that much. I get to the shrubbery around the water, and almost to the path that leads out of here. And then I hear his breath behind me, grating and awful, and his hand goes to my hair again, and I know it's going to be bad this time.

I punched him in the groin. It can't be anything *but* bad.

In fact, it's much worse. He doesn't just yank me down to the ground or drag me back to the apartment, kicking and screaming. I catch a glimpse of his face, and he isn't even human anymore. He's not real. He's just a thing who yanks me by my hair, until I'm suddenly floundering, falling, with the taste of chlorine in my mouth.

I'm in the water, I think, but such inane announcements from my brain don't help me. I need my brain to do something else, quick – formulate an escape plan maybe, or remind me how to swim so I can get away. But it's too slow on the uptake. It just about registers that I'm in the water, and then I'm suddenly plunged underneath it. Liquid fills my nose and stings my eyes; it floods my mouth before I can stop it.

How could I have stopped it? How could I have expected this?

He's going to drown me, I think, and then a second or two later that nightmarish fantasy turns into something real. I can't breathe. He's got his hand on the top of my head, and I can't breathe. I can't even prise him away with my flapping, fighting hands, because I'm half blind and still in shock and, oh God, everything is going fuzzy.

Everything is going fuzzy really, really fast, which I suppose is a relief in one way. For a second there, I was really panicked and heartbroken, and no one enjoys feeling like that before they die. I much prefer this kind of odd calm, and the lasting image of all of this neon blue floating around me, as I drift away.

My life doesn't flash before my eyes, but that's OK. My life wasn't anything to speak of anyway. It was dull and monotonous, with the occasional violent episode. The occasional brilliant moment, when Ivan wrote those words out for me: *my thoughts turn to you.*

My thoughts turn to you, my immortal beloved, I think, and then my mouth is suddenly full of salt, amidst the chlorine. I'm not sad. I wouldn't want you to think I was. I'm happy that my last thought is of something so lovely and romantic it couldn't possibly be real. I probably made him up, my Ivan.

I made him up, which is why the pressure on my head suddenly eases. I'm dreaming of him coming for me, of saving me, even though he can't. He's not real. I'm just imagining that sudden loss of the hand on top of my head. And I can't hear the muffled sounds of a struggle, the muffled sounds of angry words and even angrier actions.

I think I fantasise about flesh hitting flesh, and the slow red trail of blood making its way through water. And then there's a rushing feeling that's probably me ascending to heaven. Or me descending to hell.

Either way, it's very bright and very fast, and once it's over there's a dark figure crouched over me. The devil, I think, but everything is so cold it can't possibly be. I'm cold all over my outsides, and cold all over my insides, too, and not even the shroud he puts around my shoulders can stop it.

Not even the sound of his voice can stop it, or the words he says that I'm sure I've misheard: *Come back to me, Abbie. Come back. Come back.*

But his kiss … yeah, his kiss makes a difference. All of that cold rushes out of my body in one big glut, and then of course I realise what all of this is. My lungs were full of water, and now I'm spitting it all back up. He breathed air back into my lungs, and now I'm alive. I'm alive.

And he's holding me. My Ivan – he's holding me.

Stupid, really, that the first words out of my mouth are *I'm sorry*. He even seems to think they're stupid once they're out, because he shakes his head and strokes my hair, half laughing. Half laughing and half telling me something I never thought I'd hear.

Don't be sorry, he says to me. *You don't ever have to be sorry, my Abbie.*

And then I know it for sure: this isn't a dream or a fairytale at all.

For once, it's real.

* * *

He carries me inside, trailing water like a mermaid he found washed up on the beach. I even feel a little like that. I suppose that's a side effect of actually getting a sort of happy ending – you start feeling like you're in a Disney movie, about to be gifted legs by your bearded father.

Though I'll take what Ivan actually does over that. I'll take him cupping my body tenderly, with his eyes fixed on mine. Like he can't bear to look at anything else, as he takes me into his bathroom. As he sets me down on the tiled floor, and takes off my wet nightgown, the wet robe I was wearing.

I'm sorry, I try to say again, but he stops me for the second time. He takes my face in his hands and tells me that it doesn't matter, that he's glad I know now. That he wanted me to know, and that's why he left the door unlocked.

I didn't jimmy it at all.

It was already open.

'I'm sorry I was scared after,' he says, and then I hug him, the way I wanted to back there in the closet. My body tight against his, every part of us touching. My arms tight around his neck, until he prises me away long enough to submerge me in warm scented bathwater.

Sluicing off the chlorine feels like sluicing off my old life. He washes it out of my hair for me, and kisses it off my lips and, by the time he's done, I'm half-asleep. I've got a million questions on my lips: Where's Sid? What did you do to him?

But they all die away in the face of his neat bed and the feel of his big body sheltering mine. He curls around me, and then somewhere in the middle of the night, I curl around him, and everything is forgotten. Everything is warm, and safe.

No one can hurt you now, I say. Or does he say that to me? I think he says it to me, just as I'm drifting off. I think he tells me that Sid won't be coming back, that he hit him and that he won't be coming back, though I could be wrong. I could be dreaming.

Either way, we wake up tangled together. He's already kissing me, and I have no problem kissing back. In truth, I kiss him back as though I've been starved of him for the last three days, and what I really need is to cram as much of him as possible into my mouth. I kiss his lips, and his jaw, and, when I kiss him in crazy places like behind his ears, he actually laughs for me.

You should probably rest, he tells me, but I've been without him for too long. I don't want to rest. I want to devour him. I run my hands all over his body, remembering places I'd forgotten, like the curve of his back just above his ass. It's smooth and solid and good, and it grounds me in him. It makes me forget the taste of chlorine in my mouth, the feel of that brutish hand in my hair.

Instead, I feel him. I lose myself in his kisses, which start out slow but soon turn frantic. He's forgotten too, it seems. He's forgotten what it's like to be buried underneath bad memories, because he looks at me when he kisses me and he looks at me when I touch him.

When I run my mouth all over him, from his shoulders to the soles of his feet.

That last one makes him laugh, again, but that's good too. I want him to laugh. I want sex to be happy and light, not dim and dark. If we play games, I want the games to come from nothing but desire, instead of a thousand different things that weigh us down.

And they do. They do come from desire. He doesn't stop me when I straddle his body on the bed. I'm looking right down at him, right into his eyes, but he doesn't say anything. He just watches me, watching him. He lies there and lets me ride him.

And when he commands me, when he tells me *harder, faster, lift your hips, touch your breasts* ... I don't feel commanded. I feel free. I'm free. The blackbird has flown away, and this is what I'm left with: the hot, insistent sense of someone between my legs. His eyes locking with mine, as I take him and claim him and make him mine.

'I love you,' I tell him, as I feel him swell inside me. He's going to come before I do, I'm sure, he's going to actually let go and give in, though it's not a disappointment when he doesn't. I still revel in the feel of his hips jerking up to meet mine, those rough hands of his replacing my own on my breasts, as I climb.

And the look on his face is a picture. He looks caught between pleasure and determination, ready to give in but wanting to give me more at the same time. He's even biting his lip, which isn't something I ever thought I'd see. He's too tightly closed for lip biting. He's too restrained for what he does next:

He throws me over onto my back in a tangle of limbs, and tells me what I already know. *You're a bad girl, trying to force me over the edge,* he says, and then even better: *But you don't have to. I'm already there. I'm already lost in you.*

He kisses those last words into my mouth, skin so hot against mine I can hardly stand it. Perspiration has made a gloss between our slowly working bodies, but it only adds to the sensations that are building through me. My nipples feel too taut and sensitive to be rubbing against his solid chest, and his cock is ever so slightly sliding back and forth over that good good place inside me.

The one that makes me nuts. The one that makes me want to put a hand down between our bodies and find my stiff clit, just to take the edge off. Just to take me to that place of relief and bliss.

It's almost agony when he stops me.

'No,' he says. 'No.'

And for just a split second, I *do* think he's cruel. Before he lets me know the reason for his denial. For the way he takes my hands and puts them above my head. It's not to stop me from touching him this time. It's for another, sweeter purpose altogether.

'I want you to come like this,' he says, as he sits up just a little. Just enough to take any pressure away from my clit, and give him all the leverage he needs. He yanks my hips into his lap; spreads my legs wide. The muscles in my thighs almost, *almost* protest, but he keeps it on just the right sort of edge.

He's dominant, without being too much. Forceful, but for all the right sorts of reasons. The right sorts of reasons make me moan in delight the moment he moves just right. That gorgeous body of his displayed to its best advantage, between my legs. His two good, strong hands on my hips, pulling me roughly into pleasure.

I almost come right there and then, just at the sight of it. At the thought and idea of it – my strong man, my saviour, the man I have saved in return, taking me so insistently, like this.

'Oh yes, like this, like this,' he says, and I just nod my head helplessly. I blink, and water runs in two thin streamers out of the corners of my eyes. I don't even know why, really. Because I'm alive? Because I almost drowned, and now I'm alive?

And I get this, instead of dying.

It doesn't seem like something that should happen to me. I've been waiting all this time for my end, and I didn't think it would be anything good. But this is good. This is so good I can't even speak, and tell him in how many ways. I just arch under his touch, hands scrabbling for his.

He presses them into my hips, like I'm doing this as much as he is. He put his hands over mine and rocks into me, over and over, that same deliciously abandoned look all over his beautiful face. He's really going to do it, now, I know, but that's OK. Because every stroke is hitting just the right spot, so firmly I could faint over it.

I'm not prepared for the pleasure that hits. I can't even let out a sound to relieve some of it because my teeth have formed a cage to keep everything in. My body doesn't want to let go of this rolling, too-tense orgasm, and even after it's done I can still feel it. I can still feel it in the clench of my cunt around his still working cock. In my belly, where it began; in my clit, which still aches to be touched.

Though I scream when he actually does it. I beg him

not to, but of course he disobeys. He runs one teasing finger over the very tip of that slippery little bud, and just as I think it's going to be too much it turns into not enough.

'Please, please,' I tell him, while he gazes down at me, this teasing look on his face. This teasing, *light-hearted* look on his face. It's a revelation, and it gives me more than the thing I'm begging for.

I don't even want it anymore. I just want him to come too. I want his body to tremble the way mine is doing, and his expression to lose all of its tension. And when I lift my hips a little, when I rock against his grip and gasp his name, I get a little bit closer. Then closer still. He moans for me, and that's almost enough.

But it's not quite the reaction I get when I tug my hands free and rake my nails down over his chest.

'Abbie,' he says. 'Ohhh God, Abbie.'

Followed by unintelligible Russian words that mean just as much. I love the sound of him giving in. The look of him, the way he arches his back and lets all of these sounds tumble out of him. He looks raw in the low light. Primal.

But once he's done shuddering through his pleasure, that same strong body turns boneless. He caves like a house of cards on top of me, the sounds he's making now more like sobs than gasps of dissipating pleasure. He's relieved, I think. The way that I am.

The way I'll always be now – though, to be clear, it's not because I'm unafraid. I still am. I even say to him in the afterglow, while my body is lax and satisfied and I'm not really thinking about anything too closely.

'He'll come back, you know,' I say to him. 'He'll come back and try to hurt me again.'

But the thought doesn't have the impact it once did. There's still room for relief amidst the fear, because even if it all happens again, even if he gets me by the hair and drowns me for real, this time, I know this:

I got to have something lovely before I met that end. I got to do something wrong, something terrible ... to make a mistake and have it turn out OK. I got to make someone as all right as he's made me, in so many, many ways.

So it's OK now.

Though I don't think I fully understand what OK is until he turns and looks at me over my shoulder. His blue eyes hold mine, not covered by anything. Not veiled, not misted over. Just pure and dark and true.

And he says to me the best thing he possibly could.

'He won't ever be coming back, Abbie. Because, if he does, I'll kill him. I'll kill anyone who ever tries to hurt you, the same way you would kill anyone who tried to hurt me. Isn't that true?'

I think of the boy, and the kite, and then I say the words as fierce as any I've ever spoken.

'You don't even have to ask.'

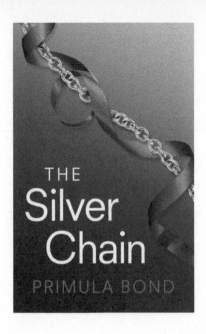

THE SILVER CHAIN – PRIMULA BOND

Good things come to those who wait…

After a chance meeting one evening, mysterious entrepreneur Gustav Levi and photographer Serena Folkes agree to a very special contract.

Gustav will launch Serena's photographic career at his gallery, but only if Serena agrees to become his companion.

To mark their agreement, Gustav gives Serena a bracelet and silver chain which binds them physically and symbolically. A sign that Serena is under Gustav's power.

As their passionate relationship intensifies, the silver chain pulls them closer together. But will Gustav's past tear them apart?

A passionate, unforgettable erotic romance for fans of *50 Shades of Grey* and Sylvia Day's *Crossfire Trilogy*.

GAME – JUSTINE ELYOT

The stakes are high, the game is on.

In this sequel to Justine Elyot's bestselling *On Demand*, Sophie discovers a whole new world of daring sexual exploits.

Sophie's sexual tastes have always been a bit on the wild side – something her boyfriend Lloyd has always loved about her.

But Sophie gives Lloyd every part of her body except her heart. To win all of her, Lloyd challenges Sophie to live out her secret fantasies.

As the game intensifies, she experiments with all kinds of kinks and fetishes in a bid to understand what she really wants. But Lloyd feature in her final decision? Or will the ultimate risk he takes drive her away from him?

Find out more at www.mischiefbooks.com

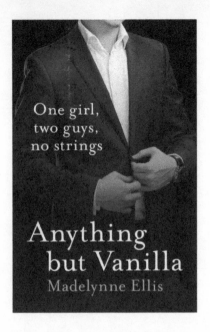

ANYTHING BUT VANILLA
MADELYNNE ELLIS

One girl, two guys, no strings.

Kara North is on the run. Fleeing from her controlling fiancé and a wedding she never wanted, she accepts the chance offer of refuge on Liddell Island, where she soon catches the eye of the island's owner, erotic photographer Ric Liddell.

But pleasure comes in more than one flavour when Zachary Blackwater, the charming ice-cream vendor also takes an interest, and wants more than just a tumble in the surf.

When Kara learns that the two men have been unlikely lovers for years, she becomes obsessed with the idea of a threesome.

Soon Kara is wondering how she ever considered committing herself to just one man.

Find out more at www.mischiefbooks.com